MANHUNT WEST

**Center Point
Large Print**

**This Large Print Book carries the
Seal of Approval of N.A.V.H.**

MANHUNT WEST

WALKER A. TOMPKINS

CENTER POINT PUBLISHING
THORNDIKE, MAINE

This Center Point Large Print edition
is published in the year 2004 by arrangement with
Golden West Literary Agency.

The text of this Large Print edition is unabridged. In other
aspects, this book may vary from the original edition. Printed in
Thailand. Set in 16-point Times New Roman type by
Bill Coskrey and Gary Socquet.

ISBN 1-58547-424-X

Library of Congress Cataloging-in-Publication Data

Tompkins, Walker A.
    Manhunt west / Walker A. Tompkins.--Center Point large print ed.
        p. cm.
    ISBN 1-58547-424-X (lib. bdg. : alk. paper)
    1. Large type books. I. Title.

PS3539.O3897M36 2004
813'.54--dc22

                                                        2003023667

For my daughter

SUSAN JOYCE

CONTENTS

MANHUNT WEST

The broken lava flanks of the canyon radiated the long day's stored-up heat with all the fury of a bake oven. Through this swelter the big rider put his clay-bank stallion at a reaching gallop, twisting frequently in saddle to scan his back-trail.

Barring him from the open gorge of the Columbia loomed a hedge of chaparral without track or opening, but a fugitive urgency made him spur the stallion into the thicket. Whipping foliage raked the man's cleft-crown Stetson, slapped his shoulders with a thorny backlash; but a series of bucking plunges put the clay-banker into the open for a view of Riverbend's clustered housetops.

The rider's body rocked hard against the swellfork pommel as the stallion dug in with skidding hoofs to recoil inches short of the sheer drop off where a scab rock ledge overlooked the river settlement.

A twin-stacked river steamer had been discharging freight at Riverbend's jetty wharf. The faded nameplate on the pilothouse branded her as Caleb Rossiter's dilapidated sternwheeler *Sacajawea*, for twenty-odd years the only passenger craft navigating the Columbia and Snake between Celilo Falls and the Lewiston country.

Beyond the packet's stern wheel, the Columbia River's turbulent flood moved like a channel of molten asphalt, two hundred yards wide. Its restless surge was paved now with a track of sunset colors, ending at the silhouetted cliffs on the west bank, with the sun a swollen drop of blood balanced on the remote Washington skyline.

As the fugitive rider resettled himself in the stirrups, the *Sacajawea's* whistle vented a plume of steam, signalling its intentions of resuming the weekly passage to Oregon. The gangplank was being trundled inboard by a pair of deck hands; a previous whistle had warned the passengers back aboard from their brief respite ashore while the crew discharged its weekly consignment of freight on the Riverbend dock.

These bearded passengers, roughly dressed with the look of Idaho backwoodsmen about them, caught sight of the horseman whose shape had appeared so suddenly and so violently on the brushy rimrock behind Riverbend. They heard the big man's hoarse shout now running toward them across the rooftops.

"Hold her, will you? I got to come aboard."

There was no mistaking the pressure of near-despair which the rider knew as he found his flight blocked by this unexpected barrier. The passengers grouped loosely along the *Sacajawea's* texas railing, sensing a break in the monotony of their passage west, put their full attention on the rider.

They saw the big man turn in his saddle for a last brief study of the canyon which he had followed out of the tawny Washington hills. Dust boiled out of the canyon's farther reaches, and the running beat of hoofs told the fugitive that John Stagman's posse would soon break in view.

He turned to rake his glance along the crumbled

edge of the scab rock, finding no break in the crescent of rocks which hemmed the river settlement in its embracing elbow.

Voices murmured excitedly along the steamer's railing as his audience realized what risks this rider now faced. Squaring his lathered stallion around, the rider nudged its flanks with steel.

The claybanker bunched all four hoofs on the ledge, snorted in protest to its rider's will, and then made the jump.

A dozen feet of free fall dropped horse and rider to the lava talus which laid its slope to the rear walls of Riverbend. Dust rose as the big stallion tobogganed on its haunches down this declivity and pounded up an alley between two saloons at a dead run.

The red disk of the sun dipped from view across the Columbia as the horse reached the wharf ramp, and the rider was bathed in its bloody afterglow as he reined up beside the boxes and bales of freight which the steamer's crew had unloaded here.

Free of her restraining hawsers, the *Sacajawea* was drifting clear of the wharfside, her big paddle wheel so far motionless while a wharfinger in a rowboat towed a drift log out of the slackwater in the steamer's path.

The horseman heard bells jangle below decks, but the packet showed no indication of putting back to the wharf. Spotting Caleb Rossiter's big shape in the wheelhouse, the rider directed his second shout toward the skipper, "Let me come aboard! I've half killed a horse to make it here in time!"

Rossiter plucked a cigar from his teeth, stuck his head out the wheelhouse window and bellowed back, "No dice, stranger. Chartered run and full up besides."

The rider swung out of stirrups, his stilt-heeled boots shedding dust on the wharf stringers. Out of saddle this man loomed taller and rangier than in it—a hard-bitten, sun-weathered man whose face was drawn with the tensions of a hard and gruelling ride, near enough for the passengers to read the rising anger in his eyes.

There was ten feet of open water between him and the steamer now. Something akin to desperation tightened the rider's cheeks as he realized Rossiter intended to shove off without him.

With a swift reach to his pommel, the big man grabbed a coil of pleated lass' rope, sorted the rawhide coils with a cowhand's competent fingers, and shook out his loop. He trotted along the wharf stringer to keep pace with the drifting packet's bow, sizing up the indifferent deck hands who watched his plight.

Using an underarm throw, the rider sent his noose snaking across the gulf of open water, aiming for the big horns of the mooring cleat at the base of the *Sacajawea's* jack staff.

A girl in pink gingham and a straw sailor hat was seated on the rusty capstan in the forepeak, apart from the rough-dressed male passengers. She saw the rider's cast miss the cleat by inches, the noose making its wasted slap on the deck at her feet.

As the slack of the rope started pulling it overside, the girl reached forward impulsively and lifted the noose over the iron prongs of the cleat. A quick grin of thanks softened the rider's mouth as he dallied his end of the lariat around a tarred piling on the wharfhead.

The bight of heavy leather rope lifted, tautened. The sluggish sternway of Rossiter's boat, not yet under power, was insufficient to curb this leverage. The prow of the *Sacajawea* yawed around, her hempen bumpers colliding with the wharf piles.

The lariat snapped like cobweb under the first direct stress of the boat's mass. But the cowhand timed his jump from the dock and his hands got their secure purchase on the starboard rail just as the *Sacajawea* floated clear into the open river.

Spontaneous cheers from the throng lining the deck applauded the rider as he straddled the rail. They had witnessed an audacious thing, and their sympathies were with the rider.

A Riverbend storekeeper on the wharf yelled after the boat, "Hey! How about this saddle horse?"

The claybank's owner grinned bleakly, waving his hand in a tired gesture.

"All yours, friend!" he called back.

The rider's chest heaved with exertion under his butternut jumper as he turned to meet the eyes of the young woman in the gingham dress, his hand going automatically to his Stetson brim.

"I thank you, ma'am," he panted. "You don't know what your favor means to me. My name's Cleve Logan."

The girl was about twenty, he judged, the curves of her body showing through the loose-fitting dress, the evening breeze stirring the rich brunette tresses under the straw sailor. Under his direct gaze, her cheeks took on a livelier color.

"I don't exactly know why I helped you, Mr. Logan," she said. "Unless—"

Logan's attention was arrested by a hostile bellow from the region of the pilothouse. He turned to see Caleb Rossiter desert his helm and come swarming down the companionway ladder to the deck level. The riverman's craggy face was purple with the ruffled arrogance of a man whose whim was law aboard this shabby river craft, a man who had seen that law circumvented.

Reaching the forward rail, Rossiter bawled an order to the deck hands who were lashing down the gangplank, "Stacey! Krumenaker! Throw that cowboy overboard!"

Excitement laid its cutting edge on the unkempt group of passengers on either side of the skipper. They saw Logan's lips flatten against his teeth as the two burly deck hands, spitting on their palms in anticipation of some fun, stalked toward the man from two angles, trapping him in the narrowing V of the foredeck.

Krumenaker snatched up a handy boat hook and launched himself at Logan, his weapon pushed javelin-fashion ahead of him. Logan side-stepped the thrusting steel point, grabbed the handle with both hands and jerked it toward himself, pulling the big stevedore off balance in a staggering forward lurch.

Krumenaker lost his footing and went down, Logan's spike-heeled cowboot smashing him in the cheekbone. Blood curtained the man's startled face as he rolled over into a scupper, leaving Stacey to bore in from the left, brandishing a chunk of firewood.

Swiveling to meet this new threat, Logan whipped the long-handled boat hook upward. The hardwood butt cracked Stacey on the side of the skull with an impact that dropped him, momentarily stunned. Having disposed of Rossiter's men, Logan reversed the boat hook in his hands and poised its lethal point like a spear, ready to cope with any following attack.

Captain Rossiter had witnessed this brief foray on his main deck with slack-jawed consternation. Rallying out of it, the riverman drew a gun from a holster under his coat and came swinging down the ladder with pure danger in his eyes.

In the act of lifting the gun, Rossiter felt his arm seized. A tall man in a fustian coat and polished Hussar boots had stepped from a stateroom door beside the foot of the ladder and his restraining voice reached Logan now.

"Hold on, Captain. I doubt if that man can swim. Riders rarely do."

Rossiter shook off the restraining grasp on his sleeve.

"So he can't swim! He should a thought of that before he laid a rope on my ship."

The big man shook his head. "Forcing him overboard at gun's point would leave you open to murder, Captain."

Caleb Rossiter curbed his temper with a visible effort. He said in a conciliatory tone, "Mebbe I was a mite drastic, Mister Perris." Then, turning to his groaning deck hands, he dismissed them with, "Let this ride, men. Duke Perris has vouched for this stranger." His eyes harpooned Logan, giving him the full brunt of their hate. "We'll settle this business later, my friend."

The packet was in mid-river now and Rossiter suddenly remembered his navigational responsibilities. Upstream a few miles the Columbia's placid run had been shaken by the combined influx of the Yakima and Snake Rivers, making this shoalwater's eddies and crosscurrents a hazard that demanded a pilot's complete and expert attention.

As Rossiter climbed back to the wheelhouse, Logan stepped over to haul Stacey and Krumenaker to their feet, thrusting the boat hook into both of their hands.

He said, "No hard feelings, buckos," and turned to meet Duke Perris' flat stare, saluting his benefactor with a lift of his hand.

Perris dismissed Logan from his attention with the briefest of nods and rounded the corner of the cabin onto the narrow promenade deck, a pair of field glasses swaying from his neckstrap.

As the pitman bars fed power to the paddles and the steamer made its reverse turn into the main channel, a sound of distant-muted gunshots and men's shouting drew all eyes back toward the Riverbend landing.

Five horsemen had reined up on the wharf, boxing in Cleve Logan's abandoned stallion. These men were discharging guns and gesticulating in mad pantomime to catch the attention of the *Sacajawea* as she sheered off downstream.

The sunset glow caught a flash of silver fixed to the shirt of one of the horsemen. Logan saw Duke Perris turn his binoculars toward that scene with a careful interest.

Caleb Rossiter, viewing this confusion on shore, bawled an order down the engineer's tube and the hull went abruptly still as the engines halted, letting the packet drift with the current.

Again Rossiter stormed down his companionway and across the deck, shouting to Duke Perris:

"This alters things, Mister Perris! 'Less I'm mistaken, that's a law posse back on the wharf. I figger they want this cowboy. I got my duty here."

Cleve Logan's face sharpened abruptly. He moved quickly aft, putting himself under the overhang of the deck, out of Rossiter's immediate view.

The *Sacajawea* boasted four cabins, two starboard and two port; between them ran a narrow passageway which Logan figured would lead him below decks or to the sanctuary of the stern.

He stepped into that black passage like a hunted animal in search of a hole, only to find it closed by a bulkhead amidships. As he wheeled at bay the entrance of the passage was blocked by Rossiter's big form.

The ship captain had his .45 palmed, the muzzle trained at Logan in the shadows. At this range he had an easy target.

Rossiter's challenge lashed at Logan down the black maw of the passageway, "Come out of there with your hands up, or I'll shoot to kill!"

The warning click of Rossiter's gun hammer was a dry, snapping explosion in Logan's ears.

He lifted both arms to hat brim level, thinking. This is working out wrong. I didn't think the marshal could call back this boat.

He took a step toward the waiting menace of the riverman's gun, when the stateroom door at his left opened suddenly and a girl wearing a quilted satin robe pushed herself abruptly between Logan and Rossiter's gun.

Her hair, its bright loose masses tumbling over her shoulders like furbished brass, brushed Logan's shoulder as her throaty aside told him this interruption had not been accidental. "Let me handle this, cowboy."

So swiftly had this thing happened that Logan stood frozen by indecision, though he saw Rossiter's aim falter and noted the confusion which this interruption put on the river captain. Rossiter barked out, "Get out of the way, Miss Waymire."

The girl cut in with a sharp urgency, "You heard Duke Perris vouch for this man. What more do you want?"

Rossiter's answering scowl was lost in the gloom of the narrow opening where he stood. Holding a wary eye on Logan—who kept his arms elevated, not tempting Logan to a rash move so long as this girl remained in the line of fire—Rossiter said, "But there's a law posse hailin' me from the landin', Opal. I figger this is the man they want."

Opal Waymire stood her ground. The subtle perfume in her hair laid its heady odor on Logan's nostrils as he saw the girl move closer to Rossiter, her retort coming with sharpened intensity. "Perris has this boat under charter until you put us ashore at Klickitat, Captain. Leave this man to Perris and me. We've lost too much time as it is."

Rossiter hesitated, his gun lowering, clearly torn between his authority as skipper and whatever responsibility he owed to the man called Duke Perris.

A pent breath escaped from Cleve Logan's mouth as he saw Rossiter finally wheel and vanish from the companionway.

Opal Waymire turned, showing Logan her full face for the first time, and he saw the tension this scene had put on her cheeks, the panic in her eyes, as she came swiftly back and half-pushed him into the open door of Cabin D.

It was stuffy in this cubbyhole, oppressive enough to give Logan the uncanny sensation that he was trapped in a cell of some sort; and he crossed the floor at once as the girl closed the door behind them, to halt beside a porthole.

"You had best wait in here till it gets dark," her whisper reached Logan above the resumption of the engines' throbbing below decks. "You had a tight call there and you've got to remember the manhandling you gave Rossiter's deck hands."

Through the porthole Cleve Logan saw the *Saca-*

jawea respond to the thrust of her paddle wheels, swinging away from the direction of Riverbend and resuming her interrupted course toward the broken lava bluffs opposite Wallula, where the river began its westward loop into the deepening gorge which separated Washington Territory from the plateau of Oregon.

Relief softened Logan's lips and tension flowed out of him for the first time since he had left the heat-punished maw of the canyon he had followed out of the hills to Riverbend.

He swung around from the porthole to see Opal Waymire slump down on the stateroom's lower berth, showing her reaction to the pressure of that episode with Rossiter. She gestured him toward a wicker chair which formed the only other furniture in the cramped cabin.

"Sit down, stranger. You'll find a bottle of brandy on the stand yonder. We could both use a drink."

Logan ignored her invitation for the moment, searching the dusk outside the porthole for whatever danger it held for him. A man's solid outline stood against a deck stanchion within reach of his arm; and Logan recognized that silhouette as Duke Perris, still covering Riverbend with his field glasses.

Without glancing around, Perris moved out of sight up the narrow strip of promenade deck. Being a man schooled to detect trouble if it shaped up against him, Logan felt no sensation of warning where Perris was concerned; he remembered that he was very much in that man's debt, and that Perris had enough authority on this river packet to countermand the order of her skipper.

Cool twilight wind ruffled the black hair laying close to Logan's temples as he finally removed his gray Stetson and scaled it on top of a steamer trunk shoved against the bulkhead opposite the berth where Opal Waymire sat, watching him through half-closed, feline eyes.

The glow of sunset from the river surface outside put pulsing highlights on the bony planes of his cheeks, limning the stony profile of his jaw and nose.

He turned then to face Opal Waymire, smiled apologetically and spoke for the first time, "Thanks. I need a bracer at that. It's been a long day."

Logan seated himself in the wicker chair, holding that posture for a moment as might a very weary man relaxing for the first time in too long a while.

The tautness eased from his long legs, encased in bibless levis and star boots. He was aware of the close attention which showed through Opal Waymire's cat-like intentness; she saw in him a man who had the ability to take advantage of the shortest interval of ease between periods of stress, relaxing as a wild animal relaxes, completely and utterly. But under that release was the alertness of a man who knew that danger lay like a tangible thing all about him, like a swimmer trapped in a whirlpool.

The girl's slightly oblique eyes were appraising him. She judged this stranger out of the Washington hill country to be around thirty. She got an impression of great strength and reserve energy in him as he shrugged out of his jumper, exposing a work-softened hickory shirt that was plastered to the contours of his chest, soaked with his own sweat.

Free of his coat, Logan revealed for the first time since boarding the *Sacajawea* that his waist was girdled by a cartridge belt and that a Colt filled a holster that was snugged down with thongs to his right leg.

Sight of that big gun drew a comment from Opal Waymire; "So you faced Rossiter's toughs out on deck without letting them know you were armed. I think I like that, Mister—"

"The name," he said wearily, "is Cleve Logan. And I am in your debt. Accept my belated thanks."

He reached for the brandy bottle on the stand as he spoke; a grin broke the gravity of his face as he poured drinks into a pair of cheap tumblers.

Leaning forward from the berth to accept the glass he extended to her, the girl said wryly, "Don't thank *me,* Logan. It was Duke's name that really brought Rossiter to heel."

Some mutual sentimentality made them click glass rims before they drank tentative sips of the brandy. As Logan shut his eyes to savor the costly liquor appreciatively on his tongue, Opal Waymire continued, "Cleve Logan. A nice name. Virile. Your real one?"

He grinned. "It will do. About this man Perris— whenever he says 'frog' around here, somebody hops and hops fast. Who is he that he cuts such a wide swath?"

She considered her reply for a moment.

"Duke Perris chartered the *Sacajawea* for this run

out of Lewiston. His weight is the one thing you could not have bucked, Logan. He must have had good reasons of his own to allow you to remain aboard. I can hardly imagine him grieving if you had been chucked overboard to drown back there at Riverbend."

Logan glanced toward the porthole again, giving every indication of a man who was no longer relaxed, who knew that in case trouble broke this cabin would be little short of a trap.

"Perris didn't cause you to face a gun in my behalf, Opal."

The girl shook her head, eying him across the rim of her lifted glass, her look holding a coquettish approval.

"You give me too much credit. When Rossiter was cornering you outside, Duke stepped to that porthole yonder and told me to horn in." She paused, considering him gravely. "You see, Duke had his field glasses on those riders at the Riverbend dock. He recognized the leader of that posse that was chasing you, Logan. United States Marshal John Stagman—an old enemy of Duke's."

Logan's eyes masked the shock this news must have caused him. The brandy was beginning to take its hold on his belly and he reminded himself to go easy before it played tricks with his tongue.

"In that case," he said, "there's no use in denying I was a couple of jumps ahead of a law posse. But this Duke Perris—what's he got against John Stagman?"

Twilight was thickening out on the river, deeper because the *Sacajawea* was running close inshore

25

under the loom of the Wallula cliffs. But there was light enough to show Logan that this girl regretted having spoken too freely before him; the guilt on her face was more important to him than the seductive modeling of her full breasts under the quilted robe, or the milky whiteness of a discreetly exposed ankle.

She was well into her twenties, he was thinking, but she had brushed against the rough edges of life on some corner of the frontier, and Logan believed that this woman had left innocence and her girlhood illusions somewhere a long way back on whatever trail had brought her to this time and this place.

"Duke Perris," she broke the silence, "calls himself a speculator. He deals in mineral rights and homestead lands on a big scale. At the moment, Perris, like everyone else on this dirty scow, is heading for Owlhorn, over in the Cascade foothills."

Logan's face was dipped down, his hands encircling his brandy glass, warming the bouquet of the rare French drink. He gave no sign that he had noticed her evasion of his original question regarding Duke Perris' past relationships with the U. S. marshal.

Emptying his glass, he fished in his pocket for a red tobacco tin and a briar pipe. Packing it, he remarked casually, "Owlhorn. That's where the big land rush is coming up in the Horse Heaven Hills. Where the government is opening some Indian lands for settlement."

The girl took a silver case from a pocket of her robe, extracted a black Mexican cigarette from it, and took her light from the same match Logan held over his pipe bowl.

"That's right, Logan. Owlhorn's land boom will be the biggest, wildest thing that ever hit Washington Territory."

Logan grinned. "I can hardly picture you as a homesteader's wife. Or does Owlhorn offer other opportunities for a beautiful and ambitious woman?"

She ignored his pretty phrase. "I ran a gambling house in Lewiston," she said frankly. "I was a percentage girl when I met Duke Perris. Now I'm heading for Owlhorn to open up the town's biggest casino—as Duke's partner."

Logan was veiled behind tobacco smoke for a long time. Finally he said, "I don't know this Washington country any too well. But it strikes me that Perris is taking a mighty roundabout way to reach Owlhorn by river boat. He should have left the boat up at Pasco and taken the Yakima stage overland to the Horse Heavens."

Opal Waymire's reply came quickly, betraying her concern over this turn of the conversation. "Don't try to figure this thing out, Logan. You'll be asking for trouble if you do. Everything about this river passage is dangerous. Don't speak to anyone else about Perris' method of getting to Owlhorn."

Logan got to his feet, knowing he had tarried too long in this cabin already.

"So Perris has reasons of his own for entering Owlhorn through the back door," he commented, and knew by the answering stiffness in Opal's face that his shot in the dark had struck home. "Well, as you say, it's none of my affair. I'll be getting out on deck. I owe

27

some thanks to someone else for helping me shake off that posse."

The girl's blue eyes changed expression instantly. "I know," she said. "Alva Ames. The girl who grabbed your rope. She's booked Cabin C, next to this one."

Logan retrieved his coat and hat and donned them. Stepping to the door, he mused thoughtfully, "Alva Ames. A short and pretty name for a short and pretty girl. One of your honkytonk dancers, perhaps?"

Opal Waymire laughed with a faint irony which further piqued his interest. She said, "Hardly. Alva keeps house for her brother, who is going to be Owlhorn's skypilot. Lord knows he chose fertile soil for his sin-busting."

Hand on doorknob, Logan grinned down at her, wondering if he had heard a faint note of wistful envy in her comments about Alva Ames.

"I've heard considerable about this Owlhorn land rush," he said. "Maybe I'll drop in at your casino one day—*quien sabe?*"

"Owlhorn will be a town without law for some time to come, Logan," she said. "A good place for a man to hide out."

"You strike me," he said irrelevantly, "as a girl I'd enjoy knowing better, Opal."

She stood up, close beside him. Perhaps it was the brandy taking its insidious hold on his blood; perhaps it was the nearness of this woman's sensual, worldly beauty reacting on a lonely man's pent-up hungers for the softer way of life he had missed. But he found himself reaching out to circle her body with his free

28

arm, pulling her close, and he saw her lift her mouth to meet the crushing demand of his own.

They were like that when the doorknob twisted under Logan's other hand and the door opened as they were snatching themselves apart.

The whiskery face of Caleb Rossiter appeared in the doorway, his bloodshot eyes rummaging this love-making he had interrupted with a busy awareness.

"Duke Perris wants to see you in Cabin A, stranger," the riverman said. "He ain't one to be kept waitin' by a saddle bum."

As he withdrew, the steamer captain said to Opal, "Lucky *I* opened this door just now, Opal. You for-gettin' you're Duke Perris' woman?"

3: $2,000 REWARD!

Logan slammed the door angrily as Rossiter ducked his head back. "It was a foolish thing to do," he apologized.

Opal Waymire's face told him nothing. "It was a good luck kiss, nothing more. You'll need luck before you get off this boat. Perris' favors come high."

He started to open the door again but she caught his wrist. "Wait," her strained whisper reached him above the creaking of woodwork. "One thing you should know. Toke Grossett will be waiting in Cabin A with Duke. Grossett is the man you must watch."

Logan buttoned his jumper carefully, concealing his gun.

"Am I supposed to know Toke Grossett?"

"A man in your position should know him for what he is. Duke has lots of enemies and Grossett is his bodyguard. But he is more than that—he is a professional bounty hunter, Cleve. Wanted men—if they have rewards posted for their capture, at least—are cold turkey to Grossett."

Logan's eyes considered her in the half dark for a moment, thinking over her warning, wondering at her motives. He left her like that, stepping out into the black passageway between the port and starboard cabins. The sour smell of whiskey in the darkness told him that Rossiter was lingering close by.

"I owe you my fare, skipper," he let Rossiter know he was aware of the riverman's presence. "How much to your next stop?"

Match light bloomed in the murk as Rossiter lit a cheroot, his predatory eyes screwed together behind cupped fingers.

"Perris paid your fare as far as Klickitat Landing. You can settle with him."

Rossiter preceded him out of the passageway, indicated the door of Perris' cabin with a gesture of his glowing cigar butt and disappeared up the ladder.

A fanwise shred of light streamed from the shuttered porthole in the door of Perris' cabin and above the constant organ tone of the river wind vibrating the smokestack guyrods Logan could hear muted voices inside.

Even as he knuckled the door panel, Logan felt old animal instincts stir inside him, sorting the hair roots on his neck with chill fingers. A man accustomed to danger, Logan was closely attuned to its nearness; and danger's acid taste lay curdled on his tongue now, its tocsin beating out a warning somewhere deep in his head.

The door was opened by a gaunt giant in moleskin pants and a Rob Roy plaid shirt. His face was a skull sheathed under a leathery mask and bisected by a formidable gray scimitar of mustache, tobacco-stained at the fringes.

Meeting the drilling, somehow hostile stare of this man, Logan ticketed him as Toke Grossett, of whom Opal Waymire had warned him.

Logan stepped over the threshold coaming and shifted to one side at once, putting his back to the wall in the timeless gesture of a hunted man. His gaze shifted from Grossett to the long figure of Duke Perris, sprawled on a lower bunk with his back propped up with pillows.

Neither man spoke. At close range, Duke Perris was as tall as Logan, an even six feet. His bullet head was covered with close-cropped red hair like fine rusty wire on a curry brush, with sideburns unbarbered and nearly of Dundrearie length. He had the ruddy skin of a full-blooded, lusty man, his cheeks sprinkled with freckles like flakes of tobacco. At forty or thereabouts, Perris had the worldly ease of a man used to authority, sure of his power and ruthless in its wielding to gain such ends as suited him.

These appraisals Logan made in his first careful search of Perris' face. So far the man had not turned to look his way; he seemed engrossed with furbishing a watch charm attached to the nugget chain looped across his marseilles vest, an ornament made of a .45 cartridge case set with a golden bullet.

"Rossiter says you shelled up my passage money, Perris," Logan broke the silence. "What do I owe you?"

Perris swung his long legs off the bunk, his brown eyes turning a muddy stare on Logan.

"Forget the fare," Perris said. "You actually owe me more than money can measure, I believe. You'd have sunk like a rock if those deck wallopers had chucked you overboard."

Logan unbuttoned his jumper and flipped back the tails to get a buckskin poke from his hip pocket. In so doing Perris' sharp eye spotted the toe of a black gun holster riding Logan's right thigh.

Logan extracted a gold piece from the poke and flipped it toward Perris, throwing a question with it, "Why didn't you let them try throwing me into the river?"

"Because," Perris shot back at once, "I think you are a man I can find use for."

"And you wanted to put me under obligation to you?"

"Exactly."

From his station by the doorway Toke Grossett commented glumly, "Blunt questions, blunt answers. Well, you two know where you stand quick enough."

Perris motioned Logan toward a chair, a wicker piece identical to the one in Opal's cabin. Taking a seat, Logan found himself comparing Duke Perris to a professional gambler. Their habiliments were the same—high polished Hussar boots, expensively cut fustian Prince Albert, the gaudy watch chain with its gold bullet luck piece. And, according to Opal Waymire, a gambler was what Perris was—a gambler who used land and legal finesse in lieu of cards and poker chips.

"You know my name," Perris broke the following silence. "What's yours?"

Logan fished in his coat for pipe and tobacco, all this while feeling the pure menace which this smokey, oppressively warm cabin held for him. He was aware that behind this speculator's blunt courtesy lay a purpose which he might, or might not, reveal when this verbal sparring was over.

"Cleve Logan."

Perris let his glance stray over to Toke Grossett. "You wear a gun, Logan."

After he got his pipe drawing well, Logan flipped his match out the open porthole across the cabin and drawled, "So do you, Perris. In an armpit rig your coat doesn't quite hide. So what? A common enough custom of the times."

Perris inclined his cropped red head thoughtfully. "So. The point I am making is that you did not choose to use that gun on the thugs Rossiter sent to heave you overboard."

Logan's ice-blue gaze taunted Perris with half-lidded, obscure amusement.

"I make a habit," he said, "of saving my ammunition

for more important game."

Perris' long, sensitive fingers were fiddling with the gold bullet watch charm.

"You were in a great hurry to board the *Sacajawea* this evening," Perris came to brass tacks at last. "It must have been pretty important to make you leave a prime stallion and an expensive saddle behind you on the wharf."

Logan took his time about answering, knowing this was the key to Perris' ordering him here for an interview.

"I'm headed," he said, "for the Horse Heaven Hills."

Perris sat down on the berth and laced his fingers across an updrawn knee. "You don't look like a homesteader, Logan."

"I'm not. The way I figure it is that the Horse Heavens have been cattle range for a long time. The ranchers running cattle on those hills won't cotton to the prospect of the government bringing in an army of hoe men to string barbed wire and plow up the sod. I think I can find a job on one of those outfits before the fireworks start."

Perris' eyes had never left Logan since this exchange of talk had begun. They shifted now to Toke Grossett, who stood against the inner door as if barring that exit.

"I think," Perris said finally, "that you are lying about going to the Horse Heaven country, my friend. I think you boarded this boat in such dramatic fashion because it was your only possible chance to avoid a shoot-out with that law posse."

Logan's face froze into an inscrutable mask.

"You look like a cowhand," Perris went on. "Perhaps one with a gun to hire. I doubt if that gun you carry bears any notches on its butt. That is the mark of a braggart or a depraved killer. You are neither. In short, as I said before, I believe you are a man I could use."

The dottle was beginning to fry in the bottom of Logan's pipe. He used that as an excuse to step over to the outer door, to knock the refuse from his briar outside its porthole. While he was doing that Logan saw that the door was locked. Grossett barred the inner corridor door. This, then, was a trap, should Perris decide to spring it.

"How can I haul your wagon," he said, turning to face this pair, "when you haven't told me what kind of harness I'll be wearing?"

Perris said slowly, "We are heading for the town of Owlhorn. By we, I mean myself, Toke Grossett here, and the twenty-eight men you saw on board—all of whom are in my hire. Owlhorn will be wide open for months to come after this land rush opens. A boom town would be a welcome sanctuary, I should think, to a man on the dodge."

Logan returned to the wicker chair.

"Inferring," he challenged, "that I am on the dodge?"

Perris leaned forward. "Does the name of U. S. Marshal John Stagman mean anything to you, Logan?"

That question was like a thunderbolt bursting without warning on a cloudless day. Perris, watching intently for Logan's reaction, saw surprise lay its sharp edge on Logan, catching him off guard.

Recovering from this brief lapse in the guard of mystery he had kept about himself, Logan said frankly, "Stagman? Well, yes. He was the marshal who missed this boat at Riverbend."

Something like approval seemed to touch the surface of the muddy pools that were Perris' eyes. He got to his feet, extending a hand to Logan for the first time.

"I'm offering you a job, Logan, because I think you are the right man to handle what I have in mind," he said. "I'll give you overnight to decide whether you want to work for me. The nature of that job will be explained after you make a decision."

Over the handshake, Cleve Logan revolved Perris' cryptic words in his mind, knowing this land promoter had left the most important things unsaid. In a way, he was using his knowledge of Marshal Stagman as a lever to blackmail Logan into accepting his blind offer for a job on his own terms.

"Right now," Logan grinned, "I'm too ganted out to talk over any deals. If you'll call off your watchdog yonder I'll be on my way to whatever passes for a cook shack on this barge."

Perris' eye made its signal to Toke Grossett, who moved away from the door.

"You'll find the galley aft," Perris said. "And I suggest you arrange with Rossiter for the rent of a deck hammock. The quarters below decks are hotter than the hubs of hell."

Cleve Logan stepped into the passageway and the sound of his spurred boots rounded the cabin and passed along the promenade deck. As his footfalls trailed off, Grossett and Perris faced each other for a long, calculating moment.

"Well," Perris said finally, "what do you make of him?"

The bodyguard shrugged. "A tough man. I'd say he's killed his man for breakfast more than once, boss."

"Of course he's tough," Perris snapped. "The thing is, have you got him pegged? Why would John Stagman be chasing this Cleve Logan with a big posse?"

Grossett reached up on the top bunk and dragged down a pair of tooled leather saddlebags. Unbuckling one of them, he revealed a fat dossier of cardboard placards, sheaves of wanted notices filched from various post office bulletin boards during his travels, and envelopes thick with newspaper clippings, each meticulously labeled with dates and geographical locations.

Toke Grossett had made manhunting a cold science, a business proposition. His saddlebags contained more up-to-date information about the West's legion of wanted men than many a sheriff's files.

Thumbing through the reward dodgers, catalogued alphabetically by states and territories, Grossett studied several before selecting one which covered the information he was after. Without speaking, Grossett handed it to Perris.

The blazer carried no photograph, only bold red type:

$2,000 REWARD!
WILL BE PAID IN HAND BY WELLS-FARGO
EXPRESS
for information leading to the capture of
"TRIG" FETTERMAN

former Wyoming cowhand, convicted of looting one of the Company's stages between Bannack City and Virginia City, Montana Territory, of a $50,000 bullion shipment in October, 1886.

Escaped from road gang of Territorial Penitentiary at Deer Lodge in April, 1887. Believed headed west toward Idaho or Oregon.

Description: aged 32, height 6' 1", weight 180. Black hair, blue eyes.

Officers are advised that Fetterman should, if possible, be captured alive, inasmuch as he has not yet revealed where he cached bullion. If apprehended, wire your local sheriff.

(*signed*)　　　JOHN STAGMAN,
United States Marshal.

Perris handed the dodger back. "It could be the same man," the speculator mused, excitement putting its flash in his eyes. "Trig Fetterman broke out of prison last April. This is May. The manhunt is being pushed west. And the description jibes with this Cleve Logan."

Grossett blinked complacently, sure of his wisdom

and his talents for spotting hunted men.

"We can easy enough find out if Logan is Fetterman or not," the bodyguard said. "Blackie Marengo's on your payroll."

Perris nodded. "Yes. Marengo shot his way out of the same penitentiary a week before I hired him at Lewiston, didn't he? Marengo should know a fellow convict by sight."

Perris jabbed a fresh cigar between his teeth and took a turn around the cabin.

"Bring Marengo here," he ordered Grossett, "without telling him what I'm after. It's barely possible even as sordid a character as Blackie might lie to protect another convict."

Grossett restored his saddlebags carefully to the upper bunk and stepped out of Cabin A into the humid dusk. A thought halted him then and he stuck his head in the door to put his slitted and evil eyes on Perris.

"Suppose I figgered this wrong," he said, "and it turns out Logan ain't this Fetterman. What then?"

Perris' thumb and forefinger polished the shiny gold bullet on his watch chain in his habitual mannerism.

"I can still use a known enemy of Stagman's," he said. "When I'm finished with Logan, he's your meat, Toke. He has the air of a man with a bounty on his scalp."

4: OUT OF THE PAST

Following the narrow promenade deck which hugged the *Sacajawea's* beam amidships, Cleve

Logan worked his way to the stern deckhouse, jammed now with the triple-decked hammocks of Rossiter's overcrowded passenger list.

A blended odor of onions and coffee and rancid bacon grease guided him to the after section of the deckhouse which was the galley and, according to a tarnished nameplate above the door, was the packet's dining salon.

He paused at this door, savoring the smells and noises of the night. The *Sacajawea's* paddle wheel was idling, for this nocturnal run of the treacherous Columbia was a rare thing for even as experienced a riverman as Rossiter to attempt.

The mysterious urgency behind Duke Perris' chartering this packet to reach his destination was no doubt behind Rossiter's departure from his usual practice of tying up at a handy bar after sundown.

But this was late spring and the Columbia was at flood crest from the melting snows at its source, and Rossiter had two decades' knowledge of the shifting channels.

The after deck was crowded with men playing poker and dice games on spread out blankets by lantern light, each game attracting its knot of Lewiston riffraff whom Duke Perris, for reasons unknown, had on his payroll bound for the Owlhorn land rush.

Logan tarried at the galley door, up-wind from the faintly nauseous odors of that place, and let his nostrils enjoy the aromatic smells of the Washington hills gliding past under the stars, like shadows rather than the solid substance of rearing granite scarps.

Logan gave the loosely formed groups of gambling men his close attention, deducing that crew and passengers had already eaten their last meal of the day; and it was with some relief that he stepped into the dining salon to see only one man at the galley counter stools, his back to the door.

A ponderous Chinese, gleaming with sweat, emerged from the galley proper and took Logan's order, moisture streaming down his jowls and dripping onto the grimy oilcloth where he placed an inverted plate and tinplate silverware.

Logan was stirring sugar into the steaming coffee which the chef placed before him when the man in the blue hickory shirt and tipped-back Stetson at the far end of the counter looked around, studied Logan's profile for a short interval and then drawled in a voice that carried the soft overtones of Dixie, "Be damned if it ain't Big Slim! I thought you were holed up somewhere in the Blue Mountain country, kid."

The soft-voiced greeting brought Logan spinning around on his stool, startled enough to slosh scalding coffee over his fingers. His glance raked the other man's weather-bronzed face and faintly stubbled jaw.

"Tex Kinevan!" Logan addressed this man out of his obscure past, reaching out to meet the other's extended hand over the vacant stools between them. "It's a small world, you old mossy-horn!"

Kinevan slid his dishes over to the stool next to Logan's, old memories putting a glow on his features.

"Nice to see you after these years since Wyomin', Slim. What brings you on this stinkin' tub?"

41

Something in Logan's look caused Tex Kinevan to draw back, knowing he had said the wrong thing.

"I ain't glad to see you, Tex. You never saw me before, understand that? You never saw me before."

Kinevan grinned, abashed by this low-voiced outburst.

"Sure, sure," he said hastily, and bent over his half-finished steak as the cook waddled in with a bowl of greasy soup for Logan. "I never laid eyes on you, kid."

Logan broke soggy crackers into the soup and tasted the unsavory fluid with a wry grimace.

"You one of Duke Perris' flunkies, Tex?"

Without bending his head toward the big rider, Kinevan answered, "Hell, no. That bunch of barflies and saloon thugs? I booked passage at Starbuck on this boat a couple weeks before Perris bought up the space. If I got to eat slop I won't do it with those hawgs out on deck."

They were silent until the Chinaman replaced Logan's soup bowl with a plate of fried spuds, eggs and ham.

"Still riding for thirty a month and found, Tex?" Logan wanted to know.

"That's behind me, Slim. Heard of the Indian lands Uncle Sam is openin' for homesteadin' in the Horse Heavens come June first? I aim to file on a quarter section of bottomland on Rawhide River and sink myself some roots. Can you imagine me a sodbuster?"

They had their little laugh over the picture of this old-time bronc buster plodding behind plow handles; and after a considerable silence, during which they put

42

away the Chinaman's tasteless grub, Tex Kinevan ventured to give voice to the curiosity that needled him.

"What rooted you out of your Blue Mountain hideaway, kid?"

Logan swung his gaze off the cook's broad back, busy cleaning his griddle, and decided to trust Kinevan with an honest answer.

"A marshal named John Stagman," he said, "showed up at my front gate a couple weeks ago. I—"

Logan broke off as Toke Grossett poked his head into the galley at that moment, put his brief attention on the two men eating at the counter, and then passed on toward the stern deck.

Grossett found the man he was hunting for in a poker game which was going full blast on a spread-out blanket, under the glow of the *Sacajawea's* port running light.

"Duke wants to see you in his cabin, Blackie."

Blackie Marengo, his square brute face still carrying the recent pallor he had picked up on a rockpile behind the gray penitentiary walls at Deer Lodge, glanced up to scan Perris' bodyguard with impatience pulling his thick lips off tobacco-stained snags of teeth.

"He can wait till I finish this hand, Toke," the escaped convict snapped. "I got my pile ridin' in this pot."

Grossett nodded, squatting down to size up the game. Poker was life itself to Grossett, and he caught the dealer's nod and fished in his Rob Roy shirt for a

43

roll of greenbacks, intending to take Blackie Marengo's place when he left.

Back in the galley salon, Logan dropped a silver dollar on the counter and got off the stool, leaning over Tex Kinevan as he reached for the jar of toothpicks.

"That's the way my cards lay," Logan said. "Reckon you're the only man living I'd tell my story to. You can see why I don't want anybody on this steamer knowing we're friends."

Kinevan regarded his slab of pie gloomily, then eyed his old friend under the curled brim of his Stetson, considerably disturbed by the things Logan had confided in him.

"Sure, sure. A man in your position can't play it too safe. I wouldn't bet a plugged nickel on you bein' alive this time next week, though."

Logan left the deckhouse, his jaded weariness assuaged by this first food he had had since daybreak, back in the Touchet Hills. That meal had been gulped down in saddle.

He crossed to the starboard promenade deck, squinting up at the dim glow of the binnacle light in the pilothouse where Caleb Rossiter's big shape was crouched behind the wheel, eyes boring into the black mystery of the river gorge ahead.

He glanced at the boiling tide of the river alongside the hull and knew he was trapped aboard the *Sacajawea*; even an experienced swimmer would be lost trying to buck those twisting currents to reach the near bank, and Cleve Logan had a rider's natural dread of water.

Shouldering past the dangling hammocks, some of them sagged by the bulk of sleepers who had turned in early, Logan was reminded of what Duke Perris had told him about seeing the skipper and renting a hammock for the night.

He thought of Perris' mysterious offer of a job, and knew he would be ten times a reckless fool to accept it sight unseen; and again he felt the trapped feeling of being a man whose destiny had gotten out of control, forcing him into being a pawn for whatever Perris might have in mind for him.

The natural run of his thoughts brought him to Opal Waymire, and what the honkytonk girl had told him about Alva Ames.

Save for their brief exchange of words at the moment of his leaping from the Riverbend dock to the bow of this packet, Logan had had no other contact with the girl in pink gingham. Opal had said she occupied the cabin next to D, and Logan found himself heading that way now.

He paused at the outer door of Alva's stateroom, hearing the girl's voice inside. She was reading aloud from the Psalms, and at intervals Logan heard a man's voice break into the reading to comment on some phase of Scriptural interpretation.

That would be Alva's brother, most likely; the man of God who, knowing Owlhorn would shortly become the devil's playground, was headed for that boom camp to carry the Gospel to its sinners.

Logan reached a fist toward the door with the intention of knocking, when he realized that Alva Ames' brother was at prayer; that this would be an awkward time to invade their privacy.

He turned away, packing his pipe thoughtfully, his mind dwelling on the brand of courage it took to be a preacher in a Godless land. He plumbed his jumper pocket for a match and was shielding his face from the wind while he lighted his pipe when he heard the scrape of a man's boots moving up the narrow deckway behind him.

Logan turned into the wind, still holding the match over his pipe bowl, and was watching the formless shape of the approaching man when that individual crossed the bar of lamplight from Opal's cabin.

Sight of that bald nutshell head and bull neck was a physical shock to Logan as, for the second time aboard the *Sacajawea* tonight, he found himself facing someone out of his past. He told himself this could not be; but he had to be sure and so he spoke a name softly at the looming bulk before him, "Marengo?"

The big shape halted as if he had struck an invisible wall and fell back a step, taking his close-up look at Cleve Logan's face, dim but plain enough in the reflected lamplight from the Ames' porthole.

Blackie Marengo's jaw sagged to expose his dirty snags of teeth. Pure shock was limned in the convict's blocky features as he lurched back still another step, the point of his shoulder rubbing the cabin wall, recognition bulging his bloodshot eyeballs.

"By God, it's Cleve Logan!"

The words ground out of the depths of Blackie Marengo's chest like a mutter of thunder far back in some mountain canyon. He added in a softer tone, "I been hopin' our trails would cross."

In that instant Logan knew with blinding surety that this man intended to kill him. It was written in the sudden clamp of Marengo's teeth, in the furtive way his hand poised at the open lapels of his coat.

Marengo had lost none of his festering hate since that day, two years back, when these two had faced the warden of Montana's penitentiary.

There was no time for preliminaries between these two, meeting so unexpectedly and at such short range. Like bear and bull trapped in the game pit, they lunged at each other, Logan concentrating on seizing the hand Marengo had stabbed under his coat.

He got his grip on Marengo's thick wrist and forearm as they collided with breath-jarring impact. Logan was outweighed by fifty pounds and he carried scars on his body which this rock-crusher of a giant had inflicted on him in the past.

Twisting, Marengo clubbed Logan's kidneys with his free fist. Logan hurled his full weight on the hold he had on the man's other arm; his right leg came between Marengo's knees and they went down on the narrow deck, rolling as Marengo wrenched his pinioned arm away from his body.

In the dim light of that deckway Logan saw that Blackie's great fist clutched a knife. Logan forced that hand back, using his lifting weight for leverage to

47

twist Marengo's elbow behind his back before the big fellow could regain his balance.

White heat flowed through Logan's back from the sledging blows he was taking; they writhed to their feet, boots grinding on the splintery deck, as Logan doubled Marengo's trapped arm higher behind his shoulder blades.

Bone bent under Marengo's muscles, bent beyond his endurance and snapped like a breaking twig before Marengo could bawl out either in pain or submission; and the knife fell to the deck at their feet.

Logan released his grip on that broken, useless arm and broke clear, yanking at his jumper to clear his gun, knowing he must brain Marengo before their fight attracted attention.

So far their clash had been in silence, but that could not last; and for Logan, discovery would be fatal.

Marengo wheeled completely around, his dangling arm a dead weight in its socket. But he squatted to avoid the whistling arc of the gun barrel in Logan's fist and his good hand, bracing him off the deck, seized the bowie knife he had dropped.

As Logan set himself for another attempt at clubbing Marengo's bald pate with gun steel, Marengo reared upwards, stabbing the knife point uppermost at Logan's chest.

Logan felt the hot bite of steel gouge his ribs, and his effort to dodge the stroke of that knife robbed his down-swinging gun arm of its full power.

The .45 muzzle slanted like the flat of an ax blade off Marengo's temple, its impact stifling the bull roar that was lifting in the big man's throat.

Marengo's face went slack then and his eyes had a queer glaze in them as Logan's blow drove him backward to strike the steamer's railing.

Rotten wood splintered to the heavy jolt of Marengo's body and gave way where the railing met a steel stanchion which supported the texas. A six-foot section of railing collapsed outward from the *Sacajawea's* hull. Feeling himself catapulting backward into space, Marengo dropped his knife and his clawing hand made its frantic swipe at Logan, seizing his jumper and pulling him forward as Marengo catapulted backward through the gap in the railing.

Logan's head smashed hard against the upright steel stanchion. Fireworks exploded behind his eyes; he was unaware of Marengo's fingers ripping the fabric of his jumper. He knew Marengo was falling overboard, and that thought was Logan's last conscious impression; his brain dropped into a black vortex into which pain and fear and all sensations were nothing.

Marengo's hurtling body made a great splashing geyser alongside the *Sacajawea's* hull, vanished in the frothy wake of the paddle wheel. Only the stanchion pillar which had knocked him out had prevented Cleve Logan from following the convict into that watery doom.

Logan was sprawled on the cramped deck when Alva Ames stepped out of her cabin to investigate the sound of combat there, the lamplight streaming past her to lay its glitter on the welling blood which spread across the front of Logan's shirt.

Cleve Logan opened his eyes from a natural sleep to find himself stretched full length on a cabin berth. Morning's first light showed pearl-rose beyond a circle of glass port. For a long moment he lay there, puzzled as to where he was or how he got here, trying to pick up the broken thread of memory.

Then a woman's soft voice impinged itself on his consciousness, near at hand. He thought instantly of Opal Waymire and wondered by what freak of circumstance he had wound up in Cabin D.

But it was Alva Ames whose face he saw when he turned his head on the pillow. She was kneeling beside the berth, her face showing the strain of a sleepless night.

"I think you have nothing to worry about, Mr. Logan," she was saying. "The knife wound was shallow and you were not unconscious long from the blow on your skull. You drifted into a sound natural sleep shortly after Jeb carried you in here."

Logan groped a hand to his skull, aware that his head had a slugging ache in it which seemed oddly out of accord with his general sense of refreshment and bodily well-being.

His fingers brushed over an egg-sized welt where his scalp had made contact with the iron stanchion outside, and with that discovery Cleve Logan remembered the fight, remembered seeing Blackie Marengo drop toward the treacherous waters of the swollen Columbia.

He thought, Blackie had a broken arm. He never had a chance in that river, which means my secret is safe.

Logan sat up, promptly thumping his sore head against the rawhide springs of the upper berth. He swung his legs from under the blanket that covered him and saw that he still wore his levis but that his socks and cowboots had been removed.

Glancing down, he saw that he was shirtless as well. His chest was bound in tightly-wound strips of bandage, torn from a petticoat or a bedsheet. Under that bandage was a steady pulsing ache where Marengo's knife had sliced its shallow track.

Logan managed a crooked grin.

"Looks like I'm in your debt again, Miss Ames," he said. "What happened?"

A softly modulated male voice answered him from the far part of the stateroom. "My sister and I heard your fight with Blackie Marengo. When it was over we brought you in here. God had you in the hollow of His hand last night, Mr. Logan."

Logan turned to get his first look at Alva's brother. Ames was younger than he had expected—in his middle twenties—and he wore the reversed collar and black garb of a frontier clergyman.

The minister's sun-weathered, intensely vital face would have been handsome had it not been for a patch of puckered scar tissue which covered his forehead and drew his entire left cheek out of shape.

With a start, Cleve Logan realized that the man was stone blind. His eyes, lusterless behind scarred lids,

51

had the opaque fixity of a sightless person.

"My brother," Alva said. "Reverend Jebediah Ames."

The blind man reached a hand in Logan's direction and his grip was strong and sure and virile.

"This is a pleasure," Logan said gently. "Does the captain know about my tangle with Marengo?"

Jebediah Ames' sightless gaze focused somewhere past Logan as he shook his head.

"We saw no reason to give Rossiter further cause to be antagonistic toward you, Mr. Logan. You see, my sister and I knew of this Blackie Marengo back in Lewiston, before he went to jail and when he used another name. His death is the vengeance of the Lord. I pray you not to let his drowning last night trouble your conscience."

Cleve Logan's mind was busy as he donned his socks and boots and shirt. When Alva handed him his riding jumper he noticed that the girl had neatly mended the tear made by Blackie Marengo's clutching fingers.

His gun harness hung from a peg on the corner post of the bunk; he saw the girl's attention fixed on him as he buckled on the shell belt and thonged the holster in place on his thigh.

Force of habit made him remove the Colt from scabbard and give the loaded chambers a brief inspection, putting the empty chamber under the firing pin before restoring it to holster.

"I'm glad you knew the smell of skunk Blackie Marengo carried," Logan said. "I didn't throw him

52

overboard, actually."

The girl averted her eyes. "As Jeb said, his loss is nothing to grieve."

Logan stepped to the promenade door and opened it, taking his exploratory look outside. The *Sacajawea's* stacks were pouring white smoke, the packet having come into the main seaward-rushing run of the Columbia during the night.

Fifty yards off the starboard beam the high eroded bluffs of Washington Territory lay green and fertile under the dawning sun, giving no hint of the desert aridity to which they would revert when summer came. It was an empty land without visible road or human habitation along its southern border. The Oregon plateau lay across the river at this point, a quarter of a mile south; Logan judged that high noon would see the *Sacajawea* tying up at Celilo Falls, the end of navigation from the east.

His glance dropped to survey the missing length of boat railing, which someone had temporarily repaired with a length of rope tied between stanchions. Someone had sluiced the bloodstains off the deck where he and Marengo had fought their silent, bitter fight to the end.

Logan swung full around, his glance shuttling between Alva and her brother.

"When was that break in the railing discovered?"

Jeb Ames answered, "It was after midnight. There was considerable hullabaloo from Rossiter. He told his crew the railing had been in need of repairs for months."

Logan's voice sharpened. "Does the captain know one of his passengers went overboard?"

"Not that we know of. But neither of us has left this cabin."

Logan's relief came with an outrush of breath. He started to speak and was interrupted by the blast of the *Sacajawea's* whistle, drenching the overhead deck with spray. That signal changed whatever Logan had been about to say.

"Rossiter's whistling for a landing," he said tensely. "I will not complicate your situation by remaining here, Miss Ames. I want you to take my thanks, for what it is worth."

He fitted his Stetson at an angle across his head to conceal the narrow bandage Alva had bound around the gash on his skull.

Over his handshake with Jebediah Ames, Logan said, "I understand you're taking over the skypilot's job at Owlhorn, Reverend. You couldn't have chosen a wilder spot to preach the Gospel."

Jebediah Ames' smile transformed his scarred face.

"I go where the Lord calleth," he said humbly. "Owlhorn needs to learn of the teachings of Jesus Christ perhaps more than any other community in Washington Territory. I thank God that He chose me for His missionary there."

Logan stepped out of Cabin C and closed the door behind him. He moved quickly aft along this deck, seeing the Washington bank quartering in closer as the *Sacajawea*, her engines at half speed, veered in toward an obscure landing dock built at the end of a rocky outcrop covered with second growth timber.

This port of call was no town, then; it appeared from this distance to be a lonely river ranch, for he saw horses penned in a corral beyond the patch of timber.

He was approaching the deckhouse and its breakfast odors when landing bells jangled in the engine room and the packet nosed her prow into the spreading V of the landing slip.

Alongside the dock, Logan saw firewood ricked in four-foot lengths along the smooth gravel beach, and knew that this was a woodcutter's camp where some enterprising settler was selling fuel for the boilers of the Columbia's river craft.

"Fuel stop!" Rossiter bellowed through a tin megaphone from the pilothouse wing, as lines were made fast to the dock. "The more o' you passengers who lend a hand loadin' firewood, the quicker we git under way ag'in!"

Logan glanced through the open door of the dining room and saw that it was jammed at this early hour by Duke Perris' riffraff. The big deck hand, Krumenaker, brushed past Logan without appearing to recognize him and bawled into the galley, "All hands out to load wood. Rustle along, you lazy bustards."

The gangplank had gone overside and the wood-chopper waited at its foot, a row of wheelbarrows lined up beside the woodyard. Men started shuffling out of the dining salon, grumbling as they came; and Tex Kinevan came through the doorway and stepped aside, lighting up a brown paper cigarette.

"Hear anything about a man overboard?" Logan

asked behind motionless lips.

Kinevan's weathered face was obscure behind smoke.

"Considerable talk at breakfast about one of Perris' hard cases disappearin' last night. They found a chunk of railin' missin' an' figger this hombre leant against it and fell into the drink."

Logan appeared to be waiting his chance to get into the mess room.

"It was no accident," he told Kinevan enigmatically. "It could have been me."

Kinevan grumbled, "I expected it was something like that. Somebody's bound to spot you sooner or later, Big Slim. Don't crowd your luck too far."

Logan stepped into the deserted dining room and saw that the fat Chinese cook had joined the men ashore, trundling firewood aboard the *Sacajawea* to stoke the packet's boilers for the remainder of her downstream run.

He went around behind the counter and poured himself a cup of coffee from the five-gallon pot on the galley stove, swigged it down and was pouring a second when a shadow fell across the doorway and Opal Waymire stepped inside, closely followed by Duke Perris.

She looked almost demure this morning, in a form-fitting suit of gray material with a pert little aigrette hat tipped across her braided coils of corn-yellow hair. But her eyes were shadowed as she accompanied Perris across the salon, and he got the vague impression that she was almost surprised to find him still aboard this morning.

"Made up your mind about our deal, Logan?"

The fact that Perris spoke openly in the girl's presence verified what Rossiter had said about Opal being the promoter's woman.

Logan shifted his glance to the girl, surprising a look of strain and concern in her eyes.

"I'll take your job," he said, ignoring the warning he saw in Opal Waymire's covert look. "I could hardly do otherwise."

Duke Perris straddled a stool, his head turning as Logan rounded the galley counter.

"I want to tell you something, then," Duke Perris said. "This is the last stop Rossiter's tub makes before we reach Klickitat Landing. There is a railroad telegraph between Wallula and The Dalles. John Stagman could easily have a sheriff waiting to pick you up at either Klickitat or Celilo Falls."

Logan considered this information with full seriousness.

"The woodyard man out there is Grover Winegarten," Perris continued. "He hunts wild horses and breaks them for market. I suggest you leave the *Sacajawea* here and buy yourself a mount. It's an easy ride across the hills to Owlhorn. You could get there as soon as I will."

While he was speaking, Duke Perris was drawing a thick roll of greenbacks from his coat. Without counting them he shoved the currency along the counter toward Logan.

"Buy yourself a nag," he said, "and keep the

remainder as advance wages. I've got a land office in Owlhorn. When you contact me there, do it after dark. I don't want Owlhorn to know we ever met before."

Logan accepted the roll of bills after a brief hesitation.

"Hold on," he protested. "You're helpin' me duck the law so I can work for you. What kind of a deal am I walking into here, Perris?"

The promoter shrugged.

"Time to talk over details when we get to Owlhorn. You better mosey."

Logan crowded his doubts out of his head and stepped out into the blazing sunshine. A group of laggards from Perris' bunch were being herded toward the gangplank by Rossiter's big deck boss, Stacey. Logan elbowed into the anonymity of that group and thus made his way unnoticed off the river boat.

The woodyard man stood alongside Rossiter at the head of the dock with a tally sheet, watching the passengers loading their wheelbarrows from the nearest rick of cordwood.

Logan stooped to pick up the handles of a wheelbarrow and trundled it down a steep path to the woodyard, putting himself unobtrusively behind a high rick which shielded him from view of the *Sacajawea's* decks.

Immediately behind the woodyard was the cottonwood bosque and horse corrals he had seen as the steamer put inshore.

No eye saw Logan abandon his wheelbarrow and cut into the trees. He worked his way along the side of

58

high pole corrals where fuzztail mustangs were feeding, and came finally to a cabin of squared cottonwood logs which was Winegarten's home. ·

From the porch of this cabin, forty minutes later, Cleve Logan watched the *Sacajawea* retreat from the wharf and swing her nose into the stream on the home lap of her run to Celilo.

He hoped fervently that he would never lay eyes on that shabby, somehow sinister river craft again; although Rossiter's sternwheeler had played a key part in his destiny, from the moment he spotted her rusty stacks beyond the roofs of Riverbend.

He thought of Duke Perris, who was using the *Sacajawea* to transport nearly thirty rough characters from the Idaho mines to this new land rush in Washington Territory; and like Tex Kinevan, his friend so coincidentally met, he wondered what Perris' motives were in gathering up those hard cases, and why he chose to approach Owlhorn from the back door of the hills.

Blackie Marengo, the man he had heard swear to kill him if it took a lifetime, had played out his string aboard that river boat fast dwindling downriver from Logan's sight. Marengo had made his try and failed, as other men had done in Logan's time; his bloated corpse would wind up in some fisherman's net or run afoul of a sandbar somewhere between here and the Pacific's saltwater.

Logan's last glimpse of the *Sacajawea* found his gaze riveted on the figure of Alva Ames, that wholly unassuming and strangely attractive woman who stood at the paddle wheel housing beside the tall and angular shape of her blind brother.

Waiting for Winegarten to return from the dock, Logan thought: Perris must have been awfully sure of his hold on me to advise me to leave the boat here. There's nothing to force me to meet him over in Owlhorn now.

Logan found himself surprised at the way his thoughts made full circle and came back to the two completely contrasting women he had met aboard the *Sacajawea*. The warmth of Opal Waymire's passionate lips on his was a remembered pleasure in him, stirring his blood even now. But of all the personalities he had encountered during the overnight run of the river boat, he found that it was the demure sister of Owlhorn's future skypilot who had made the only truly indelible impression on his mind.

He found himself anticipating another talk with Alva Ames, over in Owlhorn. For he would ride to the boom town, despite the fact that the choice of trails before him was his to make. Owlhorn was at the end of the trail he was following; the pull of it was that real and that strong in Logan.

6: OWLHORN TOWN

Winegarten was plodding back to his shack, carrying a tin can with the receipts of his cordwood sale to the *Sacajawea*, when he caught sight of the spurred and booted stranger out by his corrals, sizing up the half-broken stock which Winegarten had choused out of the back country hills.

A suspicious man, knowing the risks he ran on this isolated perch between the frowning Horse Heavens and the river's edge, Winegarten slipped into his cabin without attracting the stranger's eye, carefully stowed his can of money under a loose slab in the fireplace, and took a double-barreled shotgun from its elkhorn rack over the mantle.

The woodchopper was carrying the shotgun when Cleve Logan stepped down off the corral rail to meet the rancher's frankly hostile eye.

"Missed the boat," Logan grinned, "looking over these broncs."

Grover Winegarten spat tobacco juice into the dust, appraising the bulge of the gun under Logan's jumper with suspicious alertness.

"You're a bronc topper by the warp of yore laigs, stranger," Winegarten conceded, "but this is a one-man outfit. Best job I can offer ye is ten a week and grub for fallin' timber an' buckin' logs into four foot lengths."

Logan shook his head to this proposition. "I guess not. I want to buy a saddle horse, complete with gear."

Winegarten grounded the stock of his gun, a trader's wily instincts rousing in him.

"Drifter who sold his saddle, eh? Lost your shirt in one o' those poker games on Rossiter's scow." Getting no reply, the mustanger jerked a thumb toward his corral.

"These mustangs are fresh off the open range. I bust 'em for the plow or the saddle an' ferry 'em to the auction yards at The Dalles twice a year. Just what are you lookin' for?"

Logan packed and lit his pipe, studying the cavvy of wild stuff with a cowhand's critical eye.

"That dun yonder by the trough looks like he's got a bit of steeldust strain in him. Got a saddle and bridle?"

Winegarten produced a stock saddle with a Visalia tree and a split-ear halter. He watched Logan rope the dun and snug it down while he cinched the gear on the hurricane deck and let out the stirrup leathers to accommodate his rangy legs.

After a preliminary run up and down the riverbank beyond Winegarten's timber patch, Cleve Logan knew he had a horse with plenty of speed and bottom.

Making a deal for its sale within the limits of the funds Duke Perris had given him might take some wrangling, if he judged Winegarten right.

Over Winegarten's breakfast table they closed the deal and Logan pocketed his bill of sale—an important document in this primitive country where random riders on unbranded mounts were automatically suspect.

"It's tol'able lonesome here, river traffic bein' off since the Oregon railroad was built," Winegarten hinted. "If you could spend the summer cuttin' timber for me—"

"No dice, my friend. What I need now is some idea of the best way to cross these hills to Owlhorn."

The mustanger's crestfallen grin betrayed his disappointment at Logan's decision to hit the trail.

"Goin' to size up the government land boom, eh?" he said, accompanying Logan out to where the dun waited. "Well, son, you foller that coulee to the crest of this first ridge. Up there you'll see the ruins o' Fort Rimrock and the old army road snakin' northwest. You foller that till you hit a bobwire fence, which is the south line of Jube Buckring's Ringbone range."

Logan, sitting tall in the saddle and already sizing up the Horse Heaven slopes he had to climb, nodded to indicate that he had heard of Buckring's spread. Ringbone was the pioneer big scale cattle ranch in southern Washington Territory and its name had spread wherever cowmen gathered to swap range gossip.

"If you git restless an' cut Buckring's fence, make sure no Ringbone line rider ketches you doin' it," Winegarten went on. "These cattle outfits are gettin' perty ringy as the time draws nigh for a passle o' sod-bustin' nesters to move into Owlhorn Valley. Buckring's been leasin' that Injun grass for twenty years an' Ringbone stands to lose its best graze when Uncle Sam opens the gate to them homesteaders next week. If it's excitement you're huntin', Owlhorn won't disappoint ye."

Again Logan nodded, having heard the grim rumors which were abroad in the sagebrush country regarding Ringbone and the changed order which this Horse Heaven land rush would bring to the cattlemen entrenched in these hills.

"Keep Mount Adams betweenst yore hoss' ears," Winegarten continued, "till you reach a valley cuttin' through the hills. That's Satus Pass, connectin' the inland flats to the Columbia River. Foller the stage road north an' you'll hit Owlhorn, which overlooks the Yakima Injun Reservation. That's where all hell's gettin' set to bust loose an' you couldn't drag me within gunshot range o' that feud fer all the gold in Californy."

As Logan picked up his reins, a thought struck the old mustanger.

"You tote a gun," he said cryptically. "If it's for hire, Jube Buckring's your man. He'll need all the guns he can muster up, if'n he makes good his threat to buffalo them nesters out of filin' claims on land Ringbone figgers is theirs."

Logan touched the dun with his rowels. "So long," he called back, and put his new mount up a game trace which angled up the thousand foot reach of the south slope of the Columbia's broad right-of-way through this primitive land.

An hour later, from the lofty skyline where the roofless blockhouse of old Fort Rimrock dominated the ridge, Logan turned in his saddle to let the dun blow. Winegarten's landing dock and woodyard stood like a toy in miniature down by the Columbia's glittering flow; the ring of Winegarten's falling ax and the splintering crash of a tree came up to his ears with startling clarity.

From the site of Fort Rimrock, Logan had an unobstructed vista of hundreds of square miles of surrounding country, stark and primitive as it was during the days of the Indian wars which accounted for the founding of this outpost.

Mount Adams' volcanic pile was a truncated stump on the northwestern horizon, the glitter of its glacial ice serving as his lodestar for the ride ahead.

Further south, beyond the smoke-blue gap of the Columbia's gorge into the Cascade uplands, he saw Oregon's rugged line of pine-blackened mountains lifting to the granite-ribbed, snow-thimbled pile of Hood, remote in the heat haze of this cloudless May day. It reminded him of the Montana Rockies from whence he came, and a strong nostalgic urge went through him.

Thus oriented, the lone rider turned his dun toward the remote loom of Adams and began his trek along the dim wheel ruts of the old military road into the rolling sage hills, the Horse Heaven country that held in its untamed recesses the key to his own destiny.

The sun was westering toward its appointed notch in the Cascade divide when Logan was brought up short by a four strand barbwire fence which stretched off and away to east and west as far as the tiring eye could carry.

He skirted this southern boundary of the vast Ringbone holdings until he came to a wire gate; he went through it and rode again toward the guidepost of Adams peak until nightfall overtook him in a deep pocket in the hills.

Logan found a seep of water behind a group of cottonwoods and made his camp there, dividing the rations he had purchased from Winegarten and carried slung behind his cantle in a gunnysack. And next morning's first light found him five miles further on his way.

Half wild cattle grazing in a lofty meadow ablaze

with lupine and Indian paintbrush caught Logan's eye at mid-morning and he veered toward them with a cowman's natural curiosity to size up their ownership. Each cow trailed a fat calf, the mother wearing a circle brand over her left hipbone, put there with a red hot iron ring.

This was the famous Ringbone, heraldic emblem of Washington Territory's most powerful outfit, and of all the brands in the register the most impossible to blotch. The young stuff was not yet branded, telling Logan that Jubal Buckring was behind in his spring calf gather.

Remembering Winegarten's hint of a range war due to break next week when the Owlhorn Valley homestead strip was opened to nesters, Logan made his guesses as to what had kept Ringbone from finishing its spring roundup sooner. Jube Buckring, reading the writing on the wall, had probably kept his crew close to headquarters, marshalling his strength for the showdown to come.

Noon's blistering heat found Logan dipping down into a greener valley where occasional pine trees outposted the vast, unbroken forests which clad the western third of the Territory. The platinum glitter of a river meandered its way toward the Columbia here, and Logan knew he had reached Satus Pass.

A well-traveled wagon road cut across the Horse Heavens in the pit of this valley and Cleve Logan knew that along those ruts stages ran, connecting the interior with Klickitat Landing on the Columbia. This road would be the one which Duke Perris and the other passengers from the *Sacajawea* would be taking to approach Owlhorn from the southwest.

Because he was in no particular hurry, Logan camped that night at a line camp of the Ringbone outfit, finding it deserted but with a stock of canned goods and a slab of smoked bacon in the pantry locker.

Next morning he left a silver dollar on the shelf to pay for the grub he had consumed, and headed up to the summit and on down the far slope of Satus Pass before the full heat of the new day struck him.

At two o'clock he passed a southbound stage dragging its gray boil of volcanic dust for miles behind it; the driver and his shotgun guard were the first human beings Logan had seen in this vast, empty corner of the Territory since leaving Winegarten's place on the river.

It was nearing sundown when Logan followed the ribbon of the stage road to the crest of a last hogback ridge and saw before him the roofs of Owlhorn squatting against a background of the broad valley which had once been set aside for the perpetual use of the Yakima tribe.

This was the country which the government was to throw open a week from now to the great army of land hunters that would convert Owlhorn into the Territory's latest boom camp.

Dominating the little settlement below was the weather-grayed spire of a church, its shingled angles showing bald spots and the ravages of woodpeckers around its belfry.

Sight of that steeple, bristling with corroded lightning rods, drew Logan's thoughts to the blind pastor who was on his way from Idaho to occupy its pulpit. It would be tough going for Reverend Jebediah Ames; and Alva would share her brother's hardships.

That thought gave a vague sense of sadness to Logan as he put the hoofsore dun along the road leading into Owlhorn, knowing that this somnolent little town was soon to be the focal point of grievous trouble; perhaps the battleground between homestead hunters and the solidly intrenched cattle interests represented by Ringbone and the other ranches which had a history dating back to the middle decades of the century.

Owlhorn—this town without law, this refuge for a hunted man—consisted of a double row of unpainted buildings, flanking a wide street which paralleled the course of Rawhide Creek.

The false fronts of half a dozen saloons and mercantile buildings made a battlemented effect on either side of this street, stamping it clearly as a cowtown little different from a hundred other cowtowns Logan had known in the past.

For years, Owlhorn had existed solely as the base of supply for Ringbone and the other scattered ranches in the further hills, a crossroads on the way to Fort Simcoe and the big Yakima Indian agency further west.

Before this year was over Owlhorn would have quintupled in size, and would become the trading center of untold hundreds of farm families, flanking the Rawhide bottomland for miles.

Already the approaching land boom had made itself felt here. As the dun crossed the Rawhide bridge on the outskirts of the settlement, telegraphing Logan's arrival with a loud booming of planks, the rider saw scores of buildings in various stages of completion, with carpenters' hammers making their industrious racket into the dusk.

Dozens of parked wagons, ranging from canvas-hooded Conestoga prairie schooners to ramshackle buckboards and two-wheel carts, were lined along the river bottom willows. The picketed livestock and winking campfires, the carefree noise of children at play, the blended odors of cooking food and stirred dust and drifting smoke—these things told of the homeseekers converging like locusts on this flank of the Horse Heaven Hills, seeking their fortunes in this raw and untamed land.

The campfires were strung along the Rawhide's meandering course for two miles or more; Logan estimated that these future homesteaders already numbered past a thousand, families from Oregon and the Dakotas and the Middle West, drawn to this far-off country by the promise of government largesse.

Hitchracks along the main streets were lined with cow ponies standing three footed and hipshot in the dust. Logan saw that most of these saddlers wore Buckring's iron.

He dismounted in front of the Pioneer House, a sprawling two-story frame structure with upper and lower galleries facing Main Street and this side road he had followed out of the Pass.

Entering the hotel's lobby with the weariness of a man who had been long in saddle that day, Cleve Logan went to the clerk's counter beneath the angle of the main staircase and informed the squint-eyed oldster on duty that he wanted to book a week's lodgings.

The clerk shoved a pencil and dog-eared ledger across the counter and turned to consult his key rack, remarking shortly, "Guests without baggage pay in advance. Dollar night, six bucks a week."

Logan scribbled on the register, spread a stack of silver dollars across the page, and accepted his key.

"Room 5, upstairs on yore left, fourth door down," grunted the clerk. "Bathhouse on this floor, bath two bits extry."

After Logan had made his weary ascent of the stairs the clerk reversed the ledger and scanned the new signature there:

Cleveland D. Logan, Kalispel, Mont. Terr.

The hotel clerk's mouth puckered in a soundless whistle as he bent down for a second look at the register.

Then, a subtle excitement rushing through him, the old man grabbed his hat from its peg, tucked the book under his arm and left the hotel.

He went directly across Main Street to the brick jailhouse. Inside the front office he found Sheriff Vick Farnick dealing himself a game of solitaire.

"He's come, like you told me to tell you, Vick!" the hotel clerk wheezed excitedly, opening the hotel register and thrusting it before the sheriff. "That's his gray nag hitched to the rack out front."

70

Farnick ran his glance down the row of signatures and pushed the book back to the clerk.

"Good work, Van. Just keep this under your hat."

When the clerk had left the jailhouse Sheriff Farnick hauled open a drawer of his ancient rolltop desk and drew out writing paper and envelopes.

Wetting a stub of pencil between his lips, the Owlhorn sheriff scribbled an address on an envelope with his halting, arthritic hand:

Marshal John Stagman,
Postoffice Box 2844,
Pasco, Wash. Terr.

7: SHERIFF'S RULE

Morning's first golden burst touched the river of silver dust which was Owlhorn's main street. The outlines of the town's ugly buildings were diffused by the haze drifting from a multitude of campfires along the Rawhide.

From the roofed gallery of the Pioneer House, Cleve Logan smoked his before-breakfast pipe and had his detailed look at the cowtown before full daybreak brought this street alive.

Directly opposite was the county jail, a low brick structure with iron-latticed windows and the date 1872 inscribed in the granite lintel over its doorway.

Further west a false-fronted deadfall caught Logan's eye because of the contrast between its sagging rooftree and its fresh coat of garish yellow paint. Ornate red letters along the gingerbreaded façade of the building informed the public:

PALACE CASINO & SALOON
Billiards — Dancing
Open May 25
Under Management
of
OPAL WAYMIRE
Queen of Songbirds
Lately of Lewiston, Ida.

By a freak of perspective, the rear of this gambling establishment appeared to have a church steeple pointing a finger toward Heaven, and Logan realized that in one view he was seeing the pitfall of sin where Opal Waymire would hold forth in tinsel glory during Owlhorn's wicked nights, while immediately behind it and up the ridge was the rundown temple of religion where Jebediah and Alva Ames would shortly seek to bring a more civilized environment to Owlhorn's citizenry.

It was paradoxical that these two facets of frontier life should thus be contrasted in such close juxtaposition; a contrast no less acute than the personalities of the two men and the two women who would occupy the saloon and the church upon their arrival in Owlhorn this very day.

Immediately adjoining the Palace was a smaller building, its new lumber showing its orange contrast to the weather-grayed drabness of Owlhorn's original buildings. Its sign held a special significance for Logan's roving eye:

PERRIS & CO. LAND DEVELOPMENT OFFICE
See us for Choice Town Lots
Buy Now and Grow Up With the
Newest City in Washington!

Another land office was further along the street, this one carrying the official approval of the United States Government. The name GUS GULBERG, U. S. LAND AGENT in gold leaf which caught the sunrise glare told Logan that that official would be in charge of handling the opening day rush of landseekers when the Indian strip was opened to settlement.

Going downstairs, Logan breakfasted in the hotel dining room and was stepping out onto the corner of the long street floor gallery when the sound of a trotting team and rumbling wheels brought him swinging around to watch the arrival of a dust covered Wells-Fargo stagecoach just pulling into town from Satus Pass.

The red Concord jounced on its leathern thorough braces as the driver tooled his four Morgans around the street intersection at a dramatic gallop and braked to a halt in front of the express depot occupying the corner diagonally away from Logan's position on the Pioneer House porch.

Easing himself into one of the hotel's ramshackle Morris chairs, Logan watched the passengers alight from the morning stage with interest, knowing the coach had made connection with the river steamer *Sacajawea* yesterday.

First to alight was Duke Perris, his head covered with a flat-crowned coffee-colored Stetson. Perris gave his arm to Opal Waymire, decked out in a plum-colored suit and ostrich-plumed hat which would be the secret envy of Owlhorn's womenfolk.

This pair headed straight up the street and turned off the plank walk to unlock the doors of the Palace Casino.

Next off the stage was the Reverend Jebediah Ames and Alva. Above the blowing of the team Logan heard the girl's voice questioning a hostler. "We'll live at the Methodist parsonage. Could you tell us—"

Toke Grossett left the stage by the far door and stepped around to the rear boot where the tender was unloading an assortment of portmanteaux, alligator bandboxes, a camelback trunk and the large steamer trunk which Logan recognized as Opal's.

Perris' bodyguard picked up hand luggage apparently belonging to his employer and new mistress at the Palace and, thus loaded, headed up the street toward the deadfall.

The remaining passengers to leave the stage were a portly drummer in a flashy checkered suit, and the lanky cowpuncher from the *Sacajawea's* passenger list, Tex Kinevan. A faint smile warmed Logan's mouth as he saw Kinevan climb on top of the stage to get his bedroll and sacked saddle. Sodbuster he might become, but he carried his cowboy accouterments with him.

"Which accounts for everybody but Perris' twenty-odd toughs off the river boat," Logan mused aloud. "Funny at least three-four of that bunch didn't make the trip on top of the stage."

Logan filled and lit his pipe, watching hostlers change teams on the stage, seeing a new driver run the Concord further down the street and halt in front of a mercantile store where a man wearing a canvas apron and green eyeshade, presumably Owlhorn's postmaster, was waiting to receive the mail sacks off the Klickitat stage.

Tex Kinevan shouldered his soogan roll and, lugging his saddle sack, sized up the Pioneer House as the only hotel in Owlhorn and came diagonally across the intersection to climb the porch steps immediately in front of Logan.

These two exchanged the briefest of looks, neither betraying the slightest recognition of the other; and Kinevan passed on into the lobby.

Acting on pure impulse, Logan left the hotel porch and crossed the street to where Alva and the stage tender were sorting out baggage. The tender was saying, "Our church is up yander on the hill, ma'am, an' the parsonage is that little shack in the corner of the churchyard. I'm afraid it's perty run down. The Lord's works don't exactly thrive in this burg."

Jebediah Ames, his scarred face aglow with anticipation as he found himself at the scene of his new pastorate, said eagerly, "Wherever people assemble in the name of God, our Father comes. The disrepair of His house is of secondary importance. If we could hire a porter to carry my sister's trunk—"

Logan cleared his throat, bringing Alva wheeling around to face him. He saw her face light up and take on fresh color at sight of him.

"At your service, Miss Ames," Logan said, stooping to hoist her camelback trunk to his shoulder. "Howdy, Reverend. I left the boat and beat you here by a shortcut over the hills."

It was a steep climb to the church which occupied the shoulder of a hogback overlooking Owlhorn from the south, and Logan was aware from Alva's animated enthusiasm as she described the sorry-looking place in glowing terms that she was almost grateful that her brother's affliction prevented him from realizing the shabbiness of the church and parsonage which was to be the scene of his future endeavors.

The parsonage door was aslant on one hinge and most of its windows had lost their glass to the flung stones of boyish vandals. But the house lost its tawdriness under the magic of Alva's fluent descriptive powers and Cleve Logan, feeling somehow unworthy in their presence, left them as soon as he had deposited their baggage indoors.

Returning to the Pioneer House, Logan went at once to the lobby and consulted the register. Tex Kinevan had been assigned Room 8 on the upper floor. The clerk on duty was not the squint-eyed oldster of last night. To him Logan put a casual question.

"This is cow country, ain't it?"

The clerk was a sour and disillusioned man. "It *was* cow country," he grumbled, "but what it'll be when this land rush starts, God only knows."

Logan grinned, sensing the bitterness of this man who, having found snug haven in Owlhorn for his sunset years, obviously was galled by the prospect of range war which would disturb the even tenor of the town's life.

"I'm looking for a spot to rent my rope," Logan went on conversationally. "Nothing like a hotel man for sizing up a new range. Know of any outfits hiring riders hereabouts?"

The clerk fixed his watery gray eyes on Logan.

"That depends," he said mysteriously. "The cattle outfits back in the hills are prob'ly lookin' for men who know more about usin' a gun than a ketch rope. That fit you?"

Logan shrugged. "Cowmen digging in to hold off the hoe men, is that it?"

The clerk waggled his bald head. "That's about how it'll stack up, stranger. Can't blame big outfits like Ringbone an' Lazy Ladder for hatin' to see Uncle Sam turn their Injun lease over to barbwire stringin'."

"Ringbone," Logan said thoughtfully. "That'll be Jubal Buckring's outfit. Ringbone packs a lot of weight in this country, don't it?"

The clerk made a vague gesture.

"Owlhorn County," he said flatly, "*is* Ringbone. Buckring runs eighty percent of the beef in these hills. Yeah, stranger, if you're lookin' for a ridin' job where you'll have to burn powder, I'd advise you to brace Jube Buckring. His headquarters are over in the Hole-in-the-Wall eight miles east o' town. I hear he's hirin' more riders than he needs for ranchin' purposes these days. I leave you to guess why."

Logan thanked his informant and made his way upstairs. Passing the door of his own room, he reached Room 8, thumped the door, and heard Tex Kinevan's gruff "Come in."

Glancing up and down the narrow hall, Logan stepped into a shabby cubicle furnished like his own room with a straw-ticked bunk, a dresser with a water pitcher and basin on its marble top, a coal oil lamp and a cardboard sign tacked conspicuously over the row of coathooks.

CHECK YOUR GUNS AT THE DESK
No Firearms Allowed Within
Limits of Owlhorn. By Order
of Vick Farnick, Sheriff.
THIS MEANS YOU!

Tex Kinevan was busy unpacking his warsack as Logan entered.

"You saw who got off the stage," Kinevan said, without preliminary greeting. "Satisfied?"

Logan leaned his shoulder against the peeled wall-paper.

"Perris' crew waiting for the next stage, you mean?"

Kinevan poured water into the cracked basin and started brushing up a lather in the soap dish.

"That's what I thought you'd be askin', Slim. No. Perris herded those hard cases of his off the river boat and up to a livery stable at Klickitat. A passle of saddle hosses was waitin' for 'em. They stampeded into the Pass ahead of the stage. We ate their dust for twenty mile."

Logan scratched his cheek with the bitt of his pipe.

"Well, they must have cut off the Pass road somewhere during the night," he said. "They haven't showed up here."

Kinevan worked soapsuds into his bristles.

"I watched the road for sign," he said, picking up his razor. "This side of the summit six-seven miles, I saw where they turned off, headin' each along a road that snaked off into the hills. There was enough moon for me to read a sign at the corner. It said 'Ringbone Ranch, 11 Mile.' That what you wanted to know?"

Silence ran its course for a long interval while Cleve Logan pondered this information.

"Good boy, Tex. Jube Buckring is hiring gunmen, I hear. That's what puzzles me. None of those barflies Perris picked up in Idaho have any cow savvy. But they don't have the look of gunslingers, either."

Kinevan's razor was having slow going over his wiry jowls. Pausing to strop his blade, the lean Texan commented, "Whatever Perris is up to, son, I'd make a guess he's supplyin' this Ringbone with gun-toters. Don't add up any other way. But those wart hawgs we seen on the river boat—they don't stack up to the breed o' cap burners we produce in Texas by a damn sight."

Logan got up to leave.

"I'm obliged," he said. He paused as a thought struck him. "You're hanging around town until the

79

government land office opens up Monday, I take it. How much time you need to scout the valley and pick out your homestead?"

Kinevan shrugged. "A day's ride should attend to that chore. I want something facing the river."

"You and about a thousand others," Logan grinned. "Kid, I got one more favor to ask of you."

Kinevan eyed Logan in the mirror above the washstand, his hand poised with razor on cheek.

"Name it, Slim. I'm in your debt ever since that tight you hauled me out of in the Bighorn country. Maybe I can help you. I got a hunch you'll need help, seein' as how you're mixed up with Duke Perris."

Logan laughed softly, then went dead serious. "Forget the bygones, son. You don't owe me a thing. Now here's the deal—"

Ten minutes later Cleve Logan left the hotel and went around back to the stable to saddle his dun. He returned to the main street, leading his horse, in time to see the big figure of Perris' right-hand man, Toke Grossett, leading a horse out of the archway of a livery barn alongside the stage depot.

The stable tender's voice carried through the crisp morning quiet to arrest Logan's attention.

"Foller that road east, Mister, and you'll reach Buckring's ranch eight-nine mile back in the Hills. Watch fer signs p'intin' to the Hole-in-the-Wall."

Grossett mounted, spurred into a lope, and headed out of town toward the full glare of the sun.

Giving Grossett time to get out of sight, Logan

80

stepped into saddle and turned his dun in the same direction, his mind fully made up as to his next move.

In that moment he caught sight of Duke Perris' tall figure striding along the boardwalk from the Palace Casino. Remembering Perris' admonition to contact him only under cover of darkness, Logan sat his horse to give the land promoter his opportunity to pass along any instructions.

Perris had seen him; Logan saw the big man in the black coat break his stride, as if debating whether to cross the street in his direction.

At that moment a blur of movement in the tail of his eye pulled Logan's attention around to the door of the county jail. Coming down the steps was a stooped, gray-mustached oldster who wore a ball-pointed star on one gallus strap. A heavy six gun put a sag in the shell belt which looped his scrawny middle.

Heading straight for Logan, the sheriff called out, "Wait up a second. Your name Cleve Logan?"

Logan flicked a glance at Duke Perris, who had paused in front of the jail office. He saw Perris' stiffened attitude as the promoter watched the lawman come to a halt alongside Logan's stirrup.

"You read a man's brand pretty fast," Logan said evasively. "What if I say yes?"

"My business to check up on strangers who disregard the rules I lay down in this town," the oldster said brusquely. "I'm Vick Farnick, sheriff of the county."

Excitement throbbed in Logan's pulse as he stared down at this rawboned lawman, reading neither hostility nor cordiality in Farnick's narrowed gaze. Over by the brick jail, Duke Perris waited and watched with unbroken attention.

"I rode into town last night," Logan drawled in the mildest of voices, "and turned in early. I haven't had too much to drink or otherwise kicked over the traces that I know of. What rule have I disregarded?"

Farnick slapped a big palm on Logan's thigh.

"You're packin' a gun. With this land boom comin' up, I've decided to enforce a no-gun-totin' rule inside the limits of this town. There was a sign tacked up in your hotel room to that effect—check your hardware with the clerk. Which you failed to do."

A faint grin curled Logan's lips. Beyond the sheriff he saw Duke Perris relax visibly.

"I get it. You read my name in the hotel register."

Farnick nodded. "My practice with all strangers," he admitted. "If you're passin' through, all right. If you're stayin' out the week, I'll thank you to check your irons at my office. That way, no temptation to make trouble if you pick up a fight in some barroom. All right?"

Logan picked up his reins.

"A wise idea, dehorning the gents who might hanker to paint your town red," he agreed affably. Then, lifting his voice to make sure it carried to Duke Perris, he went on, "Fact is, sheriff, I'm headin' over to the Ringbone ranch this morning. No rule against a man being heeled when he rides into those hills, is there?"

Farnick waved an arthritic hand in dismissal.

"I'd be foolish to think I could make that rule stick for the whole county," the sheriff said. "Wish I could.

Spare this valley a lot of bloodshed in the days to come. Well, keep your nose clean, Logan."

With which admonition the Owlhorn sheriff turned on his heel and headed back to the jailhouse, where Duke Perris had turned into Farnick's office. From the doorway Logan saw Perris' slight nod of understanding.

Curvetting his dun saddler out into mid-street, Cleve Logan headed east along the road which Toke Grossett was taking to Jube Buckring's place in the Hole-in-the-Wall.

8: TO KILL A MAN

The bitter dry smell of dust marking Toke Grossett's passage out of the valley bottom into the sage gray Horse Heaven Hills was in Cleve Logan's nostrils during the entire two-hour ride from Owlhorn.

Twice, topping a ridge, he caught sight of Duke Perris' bodyguard jogging along the wagon road which led to Buckring's headquarters in the Hole-in-the-Wall.

It was oppressively hot, even for May, and his own sweat seeped into the half-healed cut which Blackie Marengo's knife had made on his chest.

Five miles out of Owlhorn the road turned abruptly south into the heart of the hills, following a section line. From this last vantage point overlooking the valley, a long training in trouble caused Logan to rein up for a look at his back trail; and he spotted a feather of golden dust marking another rider following him up this road.

He thought instantly of Sheriff Vick Farnick, but dismissed that idea from his head. If the Owlhorn lawman, knowing his name, had wanted to hold him for any reason, Farnick had had his chance back in town.

Riding on into the sun-parched creases of the Horse Heavens, Logan followed the cuts and fills of the road between wire fences hedged with last year's tumble-weeds.

The long undulating grade led him to a rock-toothed hogback where a lone pine tree marked a summit. Here he had a vista of the infinity that stretched across the Yakima Valley, with the low-lying Rattlesnake Hills doing their sun dance to northward and the glitter of the Cascades' snow-crusted peaks limned sharply in the intense sunlight far to the west.

Passing the summit pine tree, Cleve Logan found himself in the heart of a sparsely timbered pocket which formed an oasis of sorts to break the monotony of these bleak Washington uplands.

Below him loomed whitewashed corral fences making an ordered pattern on the flats. A row of poplars flanked a lane leading to barns and a rambling California style ranch house, half hidden under tow-ering green box elders.

This, then, was Ringbone's Hole-in-the-Wall; the citadel and throne of Jubal Buckring, owner of the cattle kingdom which dominated these hills. This was the solidly dug in headquarters of the Territory's largest cattle domain, hidden away in this lost corner

84

of an arid and untamed land.

Spurring into a canter down the steep road, Logan was met by a chorus of barking ranch mongrels, loping out to meet him. The ranch appeared deserted until he reached the bottom of the pocket; then he heard a blacksmith's maul making its metallic music on an anvil somewhere, and the rattle of a cook's pots and pans in a cookhouse off across an apple orchard.

Surrounded by yapping dogs, Logan cuffed down his Stetson brim and passed into the poplar-fringed lane, flanking the neat stock corrals. Ringbone horses grazed in a twenty acre alfalfa pasture beyond Buckring's imposing ranch house; the further hills were mottled sporadically with Ringbone cattle, fattening on the bunch grass, appearing like insects at this distance.

Logan's flesh crawled with the thought that at this moment his arrival might be witnessed down the barrels of hidden rifles; he fully expected to hear the crash of gunshot and to see a warning slug kick up dust in front of his horse.

Circling away from the barnyard area toward the ranch house, Logan caught sight of a group of men lounging in the shade of a sod bunkhouse.

Their idle attitude struck him as queer for a cattle ranch at the tail end of calf roundup season; until, seeing their whiskered faces at closer range, he recognized them as the riffraff passengers Duke Perris had rounded up in Lewiston and shipped down-river on the *Sacajawea.*

The men, recognizing Logan as the rider who had

beaten a law posse into Riverbend on the Columbia three days ago and who had literally lassoed a steam-boat, waved a greeting to Logan as he cantered past the bunkhouse.

At the end of the lane Logan swung out of stirrups in the welcome coolness of the box elder shade and dropped his reins over the neat pickets of a fence which surrounded a velvet lawn as level and green as the top of a gaming table.

A curving pebbled pathway bordered with flowers riotously abloom led Cleve Logan to the deeper shade of the ranch house gallery. Climbing the steps, Logan saw a big redwood door swing open to reveal a tall, silver-haired man in a boss-type Stetson and batwing chaps.

There was no mistaking the look of authority in the bright eyes which met Logan; there was power and arrogance written in every line of this face.

"You'll be Jubal Buckring, sir?"

The big rancher nodded slightly in affirmation. Not far past forty, Logan realized that the white hair was a natural hue, and not due to advanced age.

"I heard in town you were hiring riders," Logan said, mounting the last step to face Buckring. Here the disparity in their heights was apparent; this cattle king had the physique to match his role in life, standing a good six feet six.

"I'm sorry you had the trouble of riding out here," Buckring said gravely. "Ringbone has a full bunk-house."

Logan grinned. "So I noticed riding in. Must have

finished your calf branding early, judging from the inactivity of those buckaroos out yonder."

A frown carved its notch between the cattle baron's frosty brows. "You might try Lazy Ladder, twelve miles further east," he suggested. "Ringbone isn't hiring."

Having dismissed this stranger, Buckring stepped back indoors. With the door closing in his face, Logan played his ace.

"Duke Perris sent me here, Mister Buckring."

As on the *Sacajawea*, the name of Duke Perris had its magic impact. The door reopened and Jubal Buckring stepped out on the porch, sizing up Logan with a lively interest.

"That's different. And," Buckring added after a moment's scrutiny of the rider before him, "you're different from the other misfits Perris sent me."

Buckring was smiling now, extending a hand to Logan.

"I'm Cleve Logan," the rider said. "Uh, Perris didn't tell me much about the work Ringbone had to offer. Being broke, I was in no position to press him for details."

Buckring stepped aside, motioning Logan to enter. This Ringbone living room was furnished in lavish Western style, with coyote pelts and Navajo-loomed rugs on its oaken floor, walls decorated with the stuffed heads of moose and elk, its main wall dominated by a native rock fireplace large enough to have barbecued a full grown steer.

"Perris will give you your working orders later on, I

imagine," Buckring said. "Until then, the fewer questions you ask, the better Perris and I will feel about it. You've met Toke Grossett?"

Logan's eyes, accustoming themselves to the dimmer light of this massive beam-ceilinged room, caught sight of Perris' bodyguard seated on a horsehide sofa to the left of the hearth, in the act of pouring himself a glass of whiskey from a bottle provided by their host.

Grossett glanced up, acknowledging Logan with the briefest of nods, his eyes hot-bright in their cavernous sockets.

"This man," Grossett spoke to Buckring, "ain't one of the bunch out at the bunkhouse, Mister Buckring."

Logan accepted a glass of whiskey poured by Buckring, tipped back his head and downed it at a gulp. He seated himself at the opposite end of the sofa from Grossett, closely observing Buckring's reaction to Grossett's statement.

"So?" echoed the cattleman. "Then why did Perris send him out to the Hole?"

Grossett eyed the amber shine of whiskey in his shot glass, his shoulders hunched forward.

"Perris didn't send him out," Grossett snapped bluntly. "This man jumped the boat at Winegarten's landing and must have cut acrost the hills to Owlhorn." A wary look crossed Jubal Buckring's face.

"This is strange business, Logan," the rancher said. "I dislike mysteries. You told me Perris sent you here. Was that a lie?"

Logan helped himself to another drink, aware that

undercurrents of menace were flowing through the room now. He surprised Toke Grossett's close and calculating look on him, and recalling that Opal Waymire had branded this man for a bounty hunter, he believed he guessed the run of the man's thoughts now.

"I don't cotton to mysteries myself, Mr. Buckring," Logan said coolly. "Perris told me to leave the river boat where I did, as I imagine Grossett knows."

A renewed clamor of dogs outside distracted Buckring's attention and sent the big rancher to the front door once more. Logan and Grossett sat drinking in moody silence, mutual dislike forming an invisible fence between them.

Buckring was on the porch now, greeting someone who had just ridden up. Logan remembered the following rider who had left Owlhorn behind him, and had his answer to that a moment later when he heard Duke Perris' voice:

"It's all right, Jube. Logan had a brush with the sheriff back in town this morning. He let me know where he was riding, which is why I'm here."

A moment later Buckring ushered the speculator into the cool sanctuary of the ranch house. Crossing the room, Perris nodded to Logan and went straightaway to Toke Grossett.

"The dodger, if you please, Toke," Perris said. "We might as well smoke this thing into the open now as later."

Logan and Buckring watched this byplay with the same puzzled curiosity, sensing that a dramatic development was about to take place. Toke Grossett pawed in a pocket of his Rob Roy shirt and brought forth a folded placard of dirty cardboard, which he handed to Duke Perris.

Perris, in turn, unfolded the placard and handed it to Buckring, who read the inscription thereon with a studied indifference stamped on his face. When he finished he returned the card to Perris and then put the sharp stare of his eyes on Cleve Logan.

"That has the looks of a hole card," Logan said stiffly. "Does it concern me?"

Without speaking, Duke Perris handed the card to Logan. It was a reward poster signed by U. S. Marshal John Stagman of Pasco, offering a $2,000 reward for the capture of an escaped convict from a road gang of the Montana Territorial Penitentiary, one Trig Fetterman.

Logan gave the poster the briefest scrutiny, as if its context was familiar to him. Turning to Grossett, he said in a voice that held its note of danger, "Toke, you've got the rotten stink of a bounty hunter all over you. Don't let this back you into the wrong stall about me."

Grossett's hand dropped instinctively to his gun.

"I have only this to say," Logan went on. "The reward is payable alive, not dead. I'm telling you that to discourage you from putting a shot in my back."

Grossett said nothing, his face bleached white as if every word Logan had uttered was a physical slap.

Logan turned to Perris as the promoter said softly, "We all know where we stand now. Your secret is safe with us, Fetterman."

Logan's mouth whitened. "You'll call me Cleve Logan."

Perris' smile mocked Logan. His tapering fingers were rubbing the gold bullet charm on his watch chain as he replied, "Very well. Logan it is. And now, I think, is as good a time as any to divulge the nature of the job I hired you for, Logan. I congratulate you on your patience."

A pulse hammered along the bronzed column of Logan's throat. It was cool in this room, but beads of moisture glistened from the pores of the rider's cheeks.

"You have no love for Stagman, or any other man who wears a law badge," Perris said. "Is that correct?"

Logan laughed harshly. "Come to the point, Perris."

Perris took time out to accept a drink from Jubal Buckring, and lowered himself carefully into a rawhide chair facing the others.

"Logan, I told you that Owlhorn was a town without law, a hideout made to order for any hunted man. This morning you ran afoul of a sheriff. I want you to know that I did not intentionally mislead you. Vick Farnick is a stove-up cripple who will not last long when the fireworks start."

Logan waited, tension building up in him like a steel spring wound too tightly, but none of that showed outwardly.

"What I did neglect to tell you the other night on the river boat," Perris went on between sips of whiskey, "is that the United States Government, anticipating war between the Horse Heaven cattlemen and the

91

homesteaders you saw in town, is sending its ace marshal to Owlhorn. He will arrive Sunday night, on the eve of the land rush opening. And that marshal is our mutual friend—John Stagman of Pasco."

Logan released a controlled breath. A bitterly sardonic note touched his voice as he commented, "You waited a long time to spring Stagman on me, Perris. He's the one man you knew I hoped to avoid by holing up in Owlhorn."

Perris nodded gravely. "I know that. But Mr. Buckring and I are about to embark on an enterprise in this valley, the success of which depends on seeing John Stagman shuffled out of the deck early in the game."

Perris stood up, staring down at Cleve Logan.

"That, friend Logan, is your job. I will turn over $5,000 in specie to you upon proof of John Stagman's death, providing his death cannot in any conceivable way be traced to Mr. Buckring or myself."

Logan absorbed Perris' cold-blooded proposition in stony silence. Inwardly, he felt the emotional strain of a man face to face with one of life's biggest moments.

Finally he said, "And if I don't take the job?"

Perris shrugged. "Toke Grossett is in the business of cashing in the bounties of wanted criminals, friend Logan."

It was Logan's turn to get to his feet. He turned his gaze on Toke Grossett, the sheer ferocity of his eyes forcing the gunman to avert his gaze.

"Grossett," Cleve Logan said, "you are a bloodsucking, money-mad rat. But I'm telling you this for whatever it's worth to you—I am not Trig Fetterman and you'd never collect a penny of Fetterman's reward even if I was."

Then, turning to Duke Perris, Logan said, "I hate John Stagman as I've hated no other man alive. You want him killed. Your price doesn't enter into it. I'll take the job."

9: BOUNTY HUNTER

In saddle for his return to Owlhorn, Duke Perris waited in front of the soddy which Buckring had converted from a tool shed to a bunkhouse for the temporary use of the Lewiston hoodlums. A good half of these derelicts were still in their blankets, exhausted by their night ride through Satus Pass to reach this place.

Toke Grossett, who had been assigned the role of foreman over these newcomers from Idaho, was inside the shack now, rousting the sleepers outdoors to hear what Perris had to tell them.

Scenting the moist stench of unwashed bodies, stale whiskey and tobacco fumes which emanated from the soddy, Cleve Logan shuddered at the realization that for the remainder of the week, he must share this hole with Perris' heterogeneous crew.

Perris, sensing the revulsion in the man who stood by his stirrup, belatedly offered a suggestion:

"You don't belong with this collection of rats, Logan. Tell Buckring I said for him to put you up at his main bunkhouse."

Logan glanced up at the speculator, roused from his

own thoughts by the man's hardly audible remark.

"How long have I got to lie low out here on the Ringbone?"

Perris leaned from the saddle, his voice low and confidential. "Till John Stagman shows up on the Pasco stage. That will be Sunday night. Don't show in town until I send for you."

By now Grossett had the twenty-seven Lewiston toughs assembled outside the sod bunkshack.

"All right, men," said Toke Grossett, in the domineering tone of a cavalry sergeant addressing a platoon of green rookies. "Mister Perris wants to say a few words to you roughnecks. Pipe down an' listen."

The derelicts became silent, shifting their feet on the dirt, some of them masticating their tobacco cuds, all of them manifesting an underlying nervous tension.

"You'll be spending the rest of the week here in the Hole-in-the-Wall, men," Perris said. "You'll take your orders from Toke Grossett. The important thing is, I don't want any of you sneaking off for a trip to town to buck the tiger or get drunk. My reasons for bringing you here by such a roundabout route as the Columbia River was to keep you from being seen in Owlhorn."

One of the Idahoans, a peglegged prospector with a brush of carrot-colored chin whiskers, spoke up querulously, "You ain't told us what's expected of us, Mister Perris. Some of us-uns are gittin' a mite narvous, wonderin' what the deal is. Now you got us here, how about dishin' up a little more details?"

Cleve Logan took a sharp interest in what this spokesman had said. Tex Kinevan had intimated, back on the *Sacajawea*, that none of Perris' bunch had any idea why they were being transported to Washington Territory. The old mucker's words confirmed this.

"The less you know for the time being, the less chance there is of anything leaking out prematurely," Perris snapped. "I've already shelled out one hundred dollars apiece to you, with the only stipulation being that you are all able to sign your own name and your oath to keep your mouths shut until I'm through with you."

Old Pegleg shifted his tobacco chew to another corner of his jaw and persisted doggedly, "Us-uns ain't complainin' about the pay, Mister Perris. But we ain't no-wise anxious to git messed up in somethin' afoul o' the law."

Perris' eyes snapped with impatience. "I assure you," he sneered, "that you'll become involved in nothing the law can pin on you. Just sit tight until such time as I'm ready to give you your instructions. Meanwhile, I'll shoot down the first bucko I see sneaking into Owlhorn before I send for you."

Perris wheeled his horse around and roweled into a gallop, leaving a long feather of dust down the poplar-bordered lane.

Logan saw the sullen group break up as several more enterprising members who possessed dice and decks of cards drummed up a few games of chance. Before the week was out, Logan thought cynically, the hundred dollars apiece which Perris had doled out to these men back in Lewiston would be in the pockets of a scant three or four gamblers.

Knowing of the range war which was impending,

Logan had at first assumed that these men were gun-toters whom Perris was importing to back up whatever show of force Jubal Buckring intended to make against the influx of homesteaders.

Now, watching these men resume their poker and dice games in the shade of the bunkhouse porch, Logan knew these derelicts were not cut out to burn gun-powder. None of them, so far as he could tell, bore arms. Half of them were too palsied by age or rough living in mining camps to be of any account in a fight, even against tenderfoot sodbusters.

No, they had been brought to Ringbone to perform some other function than fighters in the big deal Perris and Buckring were hatching. He recalled Blackie Marengo, who had been one of these men Perris had rounded up from the deadfalls of Lewiston a week ago. Marengo, now, would have fitted the rôle of a hired gunnie; but not these broken-down drunkards.

He put his mind to this riddle as, keeping aloof from the bunkhouse games, he killed time currying down his dun saddler over at the Ringbone barn. From a roustabout he learned that the Ringbone crew, for the most part, was out in the hills rounding up the calf crop, which accounted for the lack of Buckring cow-punchers around the home ranch.

The clang of a triangle broke up the gambling at noon, sending the bunkhouse loafers hurrying to the Ringbone cookshack. Joining them at the long table in the mess hall after washing up, a practice which no one else besides Toke Grossett indulged in, Cleve Logan felt his stomach knot as he saw Perris' men

96

wolf down their food.

Ringbone set a good table and Cleve Logan was beginning to enjoy his beefsteak and new potatoes when a clamor of dogs outside heralded the arrival of another rider at Buckring's home.

Shortly thereafter the cookhouse's screen door opened and the lean figure of Tex Kinevan was ushered inside by Jubal Buckring himself. The hum of conversation lulled as the Ringbone boss addressed himself to the Chinese cook.

"This man rode out from town looking for work, Lee Fung. We're not hiring, but I never turn a rider away with an empty belly. Fix him up with a plate."

At the head of the table, Toke Grossett glanced around, recognized Kinevan as a fellow traveler from the *Sacajawea*, and moved his chair over to make room for the new man.

Kinevan glanced up and down the double row of men who were shoveling down their grub with ravenous appetites, most of them having survived for months on the free lunches served by Idaho saloons.

The lean Texan knew these toughs by sight; but he made no attempt to conceal the contempt he felt for them. Not until he caught sight of Cleve Logan, midway down the table, did any sign of interest show in the cowpuncher's glance.

"Howdy, Big Slim!" Kinevan called out. "I thought you were over in Montana."

Like a rock thrown in a pool of smooth water, the ripples of this casual greeting flowed down the length of the table and brought utter silence in its wake.

All eyes were turned on Cleve Logan as he straight-ened up, his mouth going unaccountably taut.

"You must be mistaken, bucko!" Logan said waspishly. "I never set a hoof in Montana in my life."

Kinevan's smile faded before the ferocity of Logan's tone. "All right, all right," he muttered, staring down at his plate. "So I spoke out of turn."

At Kinevan's elbow, Toke Grossett had frozen in a stockstill posture, his eyes shuttling wickedly between this Texan and Cleve Logan, a forkful of hominy sus-pended halfway to his mouth.

He was still holding that arrested pose when Cleve Logan suddenly shoved his dishes away from him, unstraddled the bench and stalked out of the cook-house.

"Now what's the burr under his saddle, you reckon?" Tex Kinevan drawled to nobody in partic-ular. "Pass the spuds."

Toke Grossett scraped back his chair and went to the door, watching Cleve Logan head toward the bunkhouse with a long and purposeful stride.

His eyes aglitter, Grossett spun about, walked over to the table and bent to speak in the ear of the one-legged derelict: "Pegleg, go outside an' keep an eye on that walloper. Let me know if Logan goes out to the horse corral."

As old Pegleg hobbled out to obey Grossett's orders, the gunman returned to the head of the table and rasped in Kinevan's ear, "Mind steppin' outside with me a minute? I want to find out somethin'."

Scowling good-naturedly, Kinevan set down his tin

coffee cup and followed Grossett outdoors, beyond earshot of the other diners.

"This huffy feller you called Big Slim—you seen him on the river boat, didn't you?"

Kinevan cuffed back his Stetson, scratched his head. "Can't say as I did, Toke."

Grossett was breathing heavily. "That was the jigger who dabbed his loop on the steamboat at Riverbend—the one who left the prime claybanker on the dock. Remember?"

Kinevan grinned. "I heard about that. I was sleepin' in my hammock at the time."

Grossett peered sharply at Kinevan. "You knew this Big Slim before? In Montana?"

The lanky Texan chuckled. "Sure did. Punched cattle with him for a Hardin syndicate over on the Little Big Horn four-five winters ago, the time of the big die-off."

Grossett laid a heavy hand on Kinevan's shoulder.

"Any idee what his real name is besides Big Slim?"

"The syndicate paychecks was made out to the name of Harry Fetterman, as I recollect. We called him Trig for short."

Grossett dragged a hand across his mouth to hide the expression forming there.

"Go back to your chow. And keep this under yore hat. I think I know why Trig Fetterman spooked up when you spoke to him in there."

Kinevan waved a hand. "Hell, I know why he lit a shuck too. Fetterman held up a stage at Bannack last year an' drew a ten-year sentence at Deer Lodge. I figgered he must of broke jail which is why I didn't speak to him as Fetterman in front of those fellers."

Toke Grossett went straightaway to Jubal Buckring, whom he interrupted in the act of eating his solitary dinner.

"Jube, I got proof that my hunch was right about Cleve Logan bein' on the dodge. He had Duke kind of wondering when he denied bein' Fetterman this mornin'."

Buckring grunted. "What'd you expect him to do—admit he was an escaped convict? Of course he'd deny it."

Buckring listened with some small show of interest as Grossett recounted his conversation with Tex Kinevan.

"All right, so you've proved your point," Buckring grumbled. "Why bother me with this? We want Marshal Stagman put out of the way next week. Fetterman's the man to do it seeing as how Stagman almost got his rope on Fetterman over at Riverbend."

Grossett chewed on his mustache for a moment, his brow furrowing as if he were coming to some kind of decision within himself.

"Look, Mister Buckring. I got a hunch Fetterman's of more value to us than to Duke. Wait."

Grossett drew the frayed reward poster out of his Rob Roy shirt, spread it out on the table beside Buckring, and ran a black fingernail along the final paragraph of type.

Officers are advised that Fetterman should, if

100

possible, be captured alive, inasmuch as he has not yet revealed where he cached bullion.

"Ketch my drift?" Toke Grossett panted. "Trig Fetterman knows the whereabouts of $50,000 in specie."

Buckring laid aside his knife and fork and turned to survey Grossett with a growing suspicion.

"Why cut me in on this, Toke?" the Ringbone boss demanded. "You're suggesting we force this Cleve Logan to divulge where he stashed that Wells-Fargo loot, ain't you?"

Grossett's cheeks stained crimson. "To tell the truth, I'd like help before I tackled Fetterman. The man's tough and he's desperate. Even if I was after that $2,000 reward, it ain't payable if Fetterman's dead. This ain't a mere bushwhack job."

Buckring turned back to his meal.

"We better let this ride till Logan has nailed Stagman's hide to a fence. When he goes to collect his pay from Duke, we can throw a gun on him then and make him talk turkey about that Wells-Fargo business."

Grossett shook his head desperately. "Too risky. Stagman might tally Logan, for all we know. Or Logan might drag his wagon without waitin' to collect his pay. Besides which, time may be short. Kinevan recognizin' him threw a scare into Logan. I got Pegleg Cochran shadowin' him now. Wouldn't surprise me none if Logan didn't try to hightail it out of here today."

Jubal Buckring got to his feet slowly, swabbing his

mouth with a napkin.

"Bring Fetterman, Cleve Logan, up to the house," he said. "Tell him I want to see him about his sleeping quarters. We'll brace him in my office."

Hurrying to the door, a new angle halted Grossett.

"How about Duke Perris—we cuttin' him in on this?"

Buckring's oblique glance studied Grossett, knew by the crafty twist of the bodyguard's lips the true status of Grossett's loyalty to the speculator.

"Why should Perris get a cut of that $50,000?" he asked. "I'm paying Duke twice that amount for this other deal. You're the man who figured out who this Logan was. Let this thing ride as it lays."

Uncertainty still lingered on Grossett, as fresh phases of the problem occurred to him.

"We put the hooks to Fetterman today, that'll leave us with John Stagman to worry about," he mused. "The original plan was for a gunslick named Blackie Marengo to take care of the marshal for us. But Marengo got drunk and fell overboard comin' down the river the other night an' drowned. Where we goin' to find a mouse who'll tie the bell to the cat's neck?"

Buckring waved Grossett aside.

"This Stagman has Duke buffaloed, but I'm not. That star man ain't bullet proof. You go bring Cleve Logan here, Toke, before he flies the coop. This deal is too good to pass up."

Grossett found Cleve Logan at the bunkhouse playing cribbage with the oldster Grossett had detailed to keep an eye on him, Pegleg Cochran.

Concealing his relief with an effort, Grossett spoke from the open doorway of the soddy.

"Buckring wants to see you at the big house, Logan. Figgers the responsibilities you got deserve a better bunk than you'll find in this flea pen."

Logan reached for his Stetson and stood up.

"That's good news," he conceded, walking over to the bunk he had selected for himself and picking up his coiled shell belt and holstered Colt. "I never did cotton to bedbugs."

Grossett's eyes held their covert interest as he noted that Logan did not strap on the gun, but looped the shell belt over one arm.

En route to the main ranch house, Logan saw Perris' men beginning to file out of the cookhouse. Tex Kinevan was over by the hitchrack, saddling up to leave the Ringbone.

Grossett paced at Logan's side as they climbed Buckring's porch steps and entered the living room. From a door off the big fireplace, the Ringbone boss was in the act of lighting a cigar. His welcoming grin was on Logan as the latter paused, hat in hand, just inside the door.

"Come into my office, Logan," the white-haired rancher invited. "You come along too, Grossett. I'd like to get some idea in advance, if possible, about how you aim to go about disposing of John Stagman without getting yourself involved with our sheriff over in Owlhorn. I may be able to give you a few pointers."

Stepping into Buckring's office, Logan saw that this

twelve-foot-square room had no windows, no exit except the door they had entered from the living room. Toke Grossett closed this behind them.

The room was austere and businesslike, one wall occupied by the black steel door of a vault, the only furniture being a big mahogany desk and a couple of chairs.

Seating himself on the edge of the desk, the cattleman offered Logan a Cuban cigar.

"A bit rich for a pipe-smoker's blood, thanks," Logan grinned, shifting the weight of the gun belt on his forearm. "About this marshal. I figger he'll register at the Pioneer House, that being the only accommodations in Owlhorn. When Perris sends for me, I will—"

The pressure of a gun muzzle prodding him in the spine snapped off Logan's words. He heard the double click of Toke Grossett's gunhammer and at the same instant the big man's left arm shot past Logan and yanked the Peacemaker from Logan's holster.

"Stand hitched, Fetterman!" Grossett's warning sounded in Logan's ear. "You're hogtied for branding."

Jubal Buckring watched this with a spreading grin. Speaking around his thick cigar, the Ringbone cattle king said softly, "You robbed a Bannack City stage of fifty thousand in gold, Fetterman. You went to the penitentiary without divulging where that plunder was hidden, according to the reward poster. You'll tell us where that specie is, or take a long time dying with Toke's slug in your guts."

The pressure of the gun muzzle relaxed from Cleve Logan's back and he heard the scrape of Toke Grossett's boots withdrawing. The gunman backed over to the door, locked it, and braced his shoulders against the hardwood panels, assuming the watchdog rôle he had played in Duke Perris' cabin on the *Sacajawea.*

This time things were different. Logan's gun was thrust through the waistband of Grossett's pants; Grossett's big .45 was cocked and the cramped breadth of this sound proof room made Logan a point-blank target.

Ignoring the menace at his rear, Logan put his careful attention on the suave countenance of Jubal Buckring.

This was the man who stood to lose the most when Owlhorn's land boom got under way. This was the wealthiest cattleman in Washington Territory, the rancher who had some crooked plan rigged up with Duke Perris.

It struck Logan as a trifle off character, this display of greed in a man to whom a fifty-fifty cut of a $50,000 stage robbery haul could hardly count for much. Penny ante stuff compared to the sky-high stakes of the bigger game he was playing.

"So," Logan spoke for the first time since Buckring had sprung his trap. "I'm disappointed in you, Buckring. You and Grossett are cut out of the same hunk of leather. Except Grossett eats the carrion of bounty money and you had the savvy to play for the jackpot."

Color flushed the cattle baron's thick neck like mercury rising in a thermometer. Logan's words had stung this man's ego, classing him in the unsavory category with bloodsuckers like Toke Grossett.

"You've seen our cards, Fetterman," Buckring said stiffly. "We're checking the bet to you."

Logan stood there in mid-room, every muscle taut. There was a clock set in the forehead of a bronze steerhead on Buckring's desk and its ticking was like a hammer pounding nails in a coffin, to Logan's overwrought perceptions.

He saw his trapped figure mirrored in the polished door of the safety vault, the glossy metal reflecting the bone whiteness of his face.

"Without a deuce in the hole, I can't sit in the game any longer," Logan said. "The specie is in the Wells-Fargo box. I cached it under a gypsum boulder in a certain canyon over in Montana, not ten miles from where I held up that stage. That help you any?"

Buckring considered this information thoughtfully.

"You made your escape two months ago," the rancher said. "How come you didn't pick up your haul?"

Logan grinned bleakly. "With that Bannack country swarming with posses expecting me to show up in that area? Uh-uh. I was ready to wait a year, five years. Gold don't rust."

The steerhead clock ticked through the long following silence.

"I could lead Toke Grossett to the spot, of course,"

Logan went on. "Providing I have your word that that specie buys me out of this tight."

Buckring's eyes revealed their quick distrust of such a proposition, and brought a cynical laugh from Logan.

"Bed down with a skunk, Buckring, and you get to thinking like a skunk," Logan jibed. "You know what would happen. Toke would take the specie, put a bullet in me, and light out with your cut. So, where do we go from here?"

Buckring's cigar butt glowed to the fierce pull of his lips. The ceiling lamp's yellow cone of light revealed a waxen sheen on the rancher's forehead.

"He can draw us a map, Jube!" Grossett spoke with quick avarice from the doorway behind Logan. "When this Owlhorn deal is finished you an' me could ride over to Montana together and—"

The Ringbone boss silenced the big gunman with an oath. Sliding off the desk, he seated himself in a swivel chair and drummed its mahogany arms for a long, pondering interval.

"I could draw you a map, yes," Logan said. "I memorized landmarks and compass bearings pretty thorough, knowing that box was too heavy to make a getaway with. I had reason to be thankful for that precaution when John Stagman cornered me at Alder Gulch a week after the holdup."

Buckring dragged a palm across his moist temple, concentration narrowing his eyes into slits.

"A map could not buy your freedom on its face value, Fetterman," Buckring pointed out cagily.

"Grossett and I would have no guarantee as to its accuracy until the specie was actually in our hands."

Silence piled up oppressively in this lamplit room. With one edge of his brain, Cleve Logan found himself remarking the complete void of extraneous sound in this room. Its heavy walls shut out all outside noises. By the same token it would muffle the screams of a tortured man to listeners anywhere outside.

"If I've got to buy my pelt, then I'm entitled to make a proposition that will be mutually agreeable," Logan said. "Want to listen?"

Buckring looked up, his own thoughts in a hopeless vacuum.

"If you can think up something that is double-cross proof, I'll personally guarantee your freedom when the specie is in our possession, Fetterman."

Logan edged over toward the vault, turning so that he could keep both Grossett and the rancher in his view. Grossett lounged indolently against the door, his gun muzzle following Logan's shift of position. Knowing Logan for a dangerous man, Grossett was playing it safe.

"All right," Logan said, swinging his gaze to Buckring. "I'll draw a sketch showing enough landmarks to guide you to where I buried that strongbox. You have a man on the Ringbone payroll you can trust, no doubt. Send him and Grossett over to Montana. When your man wires you that the deal is okay, then I have your oath to turn me loose to drift, Buckring."

Buckring's keen brain turned this proposition over and over, hunting it for loopholes, probing it for any conceivable element of treachery.

"Meaning," he said finally, "that you will remain my prisoner here on the Ringbone during the time it takes Toke and my man to make the trip to Montana."

Logan nodded, faintly amused by the angry twitchings on Grossett's features. Grossett, trusting no man, showed the full pressure of the distrust that rode him now, putting a wide, reptilian shine in his green eyes.

"What if I double-crossed you after that telegram came, Fetterman?" Buckring asked candidly.

Logan's shoulders lifted and fell. "You hold the aces. What else can I do but make the gamble?"

The tension smoothed out the deep ruts on Buckring's face as he considered Logan's reply. He shot a glance at Toke Grossett, ignored the negative headshake Grossett gave him, and wheeled his chair around to the desk.

Pulling out a drawer, Buckring got a pad of paper, a bottle of ink and a penholder. Then he stood up and motioned Logan into the chair.

"I admire a gambler who shoots square," Buckring said with an indefinable sly quality entering his voice. "I warn you to make this map wholly accurate, your first try. I will not be disposed to mercy if my man's telegram is not favorable."

Logan exhaled a pent-up breath from his lungs and stepped over to sit down at the desk. Grossett remained at the door, his gun tipping toward the ceiling as he saw Jubal Buckring come between him and his target as the rancher leaned over Logan's shoulder.

Logan's rope-calloused fingers picked up the pen, jabbed it in the ink bottle, and made a series of wriggling lines on the tablet, his hand showing no slightest tremor.

"Here's Bannack City," Logan mumbled, "and this is the Tobacco Root Range and the Beaverhead River. Dotted line for the stage road to Virginia City. There's the relay station at Blacktail Crick. This canyon where I stashed the box—"

Buckring's hot breath was on Logan's neck as he put the pen scratching over paper. He felt the bulk of the cattleman's torso crowding the back of the swivel chair as he leaned forward to wet the nib of his pen in the inkwell again.

Drawing the penholder up and back, Logan suddenly spun the swivel chair violently around, throwing Buckring off balance, half stumbling into Logan's lap.

Completing the savage arc of his hand, Logan stabbed the steel penpoint like a dagger into the lobe of Buckring's nose.

Before the rancher's bellow of pain and fear could leave his lips, Logan had his right arm up under Buckring's chin, the angle of his elbow cutting off the man's windpipe.

The chair skidded back on its casters as Logan dragged Buckring down to his knees, so that the big rancher's body lay against his own as a shield from Toke Grossett's bullets.

With the same movement Logan reached across the desk and grabbed one of the polished bronze horns of the steerhead statue containing the clock.

All this had transpired between the measured ticks of that timepiece, a move so desperately contrived and so rashly executed that Toke Grossett's gun had not yet dipped down to cover Logan.

The heavy bronze statue had a sharp-cornered base made to order as a bludgeon. Sweeping the statue off the desk, Logan felt Buckring's first struggle of resistance wilt as the bronze base clubbed his silver-haired skull with a sodden impact.

Jube Buckring's lax, senseless weight dragged Logan out of the chair. Blood was gushing from the penpoint which skewered the rancher's nostril like a miniature arrow; the big man was out cold, his huge frame forming its barrier between Logan and Grossett's leveled revolver.

Down on his knees, his right arm still holding its throttling pressure on Buckring's throat, Logan reached under the rancher's coat lapel and found the Bisley .38 holstered under Buckring's armpit, where he had noted it this morning.

Toke Grossett's .45 made its ear-smashing concussion in the confined room as Perris' man charged away from the door in the first offensive movement he had managed since breaking the chains of paralysis which had gripped him.

He aimed his shot at Logan's half-seen head. The bullet brushed Buckring's white locks and the violent air-whip of its passage was a physical sting across Logan's cheek as the slug smashed into the mahogany desk behind him.

Toke Grossett was chopping his weapon down for a following shot which Logan knew would come without regard for whether or not it smashed through Jubal Buckring on its way to his target. This had become a primitive situation, to kill or be killed.

As he jerked Buckring's short-barreled Bisley out of holster, Logan felt the front sight snag on the lining of Buckring's coat. The garment's fabric made its tent outside the gun barrel as Logan squeezed trigger in the shaved instant of time left before Grossett's lunge carried him close enough for a sure shot.

The exploding .38 thrust Logan's hand back against the ranchman's chest, under the coat. The impact of the Bisley slug checked Grossett's forward motion, froze the thumb which was about to trip Grossett's heavy gun prong.

A gout of bright blood welled from the bullet hole punched at an upward angle through the bridge of Toke Grossett's nose.

The satanic face was shocked for eternity into a surprised mask as life's brilliance fled from his bottle-green eyes and Grossett stood there, dead on his feet, the bullet's momentum canceling the forward rush of his body.

Then Grossett's knees unhinged and he fell twisting in a half turn, his shoulder striking Buckring's inert bulk and rolling sideways to the floor.

Only then did Cleve Logan release his strangle hold on Buckring's neck. He came slowly to his feet, leaving the smoking Bisley inside the rancher's coat.

The smell of scorched cloth blended with the biting

fumes of smoke gases which eddied in milky layers in the Ringbone office, these clouds stirring slightly as Cleve Logan stepped over the unconscious form of Jubal Buckring and stood looking down at Grossett's corpse.

Logan reached down and grabbed Grossett's belt, hauling him away from Buckring's grotesquely slumped body propped against the tipped-over office chair. The clock was still ticking like a heartbeat inside the bronze steerhead, the base of which held the bright crimson smudge of Buckring's blood. Its dial registered an elapse of only twenty seconds since Logan had jabbed Buckring with the penholder.

Retrieving his own gun from Grossett's waistband, Logan recovered his Stetson and shell belt. Unlocking the door, he stood for a moment, staring through the shifting shapes of the gunpowder clouds, regarding the still figures by the desk.

Buckring was beginning to rally, his breath coming in stertorous gusts. Logan saw no point in being in this office when the rancher came to and discovered the fate of his accomplice. One thing was obvious— despite Perris' strict orders to the contrary, Logan could not remain at Ringbone.

Leaving the ranch house at a leisurely walk, Logan went directly to the cavvy corral and cut his dun out of the bunch. From the sod bunkhouse, Perris' tatter-demalion crew glanced up from their gambling, giving no particular thought to Cleve Logan's departure from the Hole-in-the-Wall.

Their ears had not picked up the muted concussion of gunfire issuing from Buckring's office.

A horse and rider waited motionless as rock images in the shade of the skylined pine which marked the outer rampart of the Hole-in-the-Wall.

Sensing this might be a Ringbone rider posted on sentry duty to watch the ranch road to Owlhorn, Cleve Logan lifted his gun from holster and held the Colt in readiness behind his pommel as he put the dun up the last steep tilt of wagon ruts leading out of Buckring's hidden pocket.

The feeling of trouble waiting for him here laid its sharp edge against Logan as he saw the silhouetted rider touch spurs to horseflesh and move out into the beating sunshine to block the road ahead of him.

Then Logan felt the relief of anticlimax as he recognized the slim shape of Alva Ames. He holstered the .45 and touched his Stetson as he rode up, a grin twisting his mouth as he put his greeting in the form of a warning.

"You shouldn't be gallivanting around these hills alone, ma'am. Especially this week. Ringbone riders are touchy about strangers trespassing their range."

Alva's smile faded as Logan reined up alongside her.

"I have always fancied that I could take care of myself in this man's world," she said archly. "If you're riding back to town could you stand my company?"

Logan twisted around for a final look at Ringbone.

He saw no sign of pursuit there, nor did he expect any. He turned back to the girl.

"It's a good idea in more ways than one," he said. "How come you're so far from civilization?"

They put their horses into an easy canter down the ribbon of road. It was the first time Logan had seen the girl on horseback, and he noted that she rode with the careless ease of a woman with considerable experience in the saddle.

She was dressed in a split buckskin skirt for the occasion; a farmer's straw hat, obviously purchased in some Owlhorn store, was tilted at a rakish angle off her glossy black hair.

"Just getting some air," she told him. "Jeb found a homesteader's wife who was a Methodist deaconess back in Ohio or somewhere and she's introducing him to future members of his flock."

She paused a moment, then said in a harsher tone, "Owlhorn depresses me, Cleve, although I almost feel disloyal to my brother in mentioning it. It's a place I'll want to get away from as often as possible, I'm afraid."

Logan detected an undercurrent of disillusion in her voice and, unable to account for that, answered, "What were you expecting to find out on the frontier?"

She turned her head toward him and he read the real unease, the growing doubt in her eyes.

"I wouldn't let Jeb know how I feel, of course. But this is not a happy country, Cleve. It's torn with greed and rivalry and the promise of trouble to come. After only one day in town, I've been able to see that."

They traveled another mile before Alva spoke again. "The people are afraid, Cleve. Even the homesteaders, who should be hopeful—you can see fear behind that hope. You won't deny that. Otherwise you wouldn't have told me it was dangerous to ride these hills alone."

Logan pulled down to a trot, remembering that he could not approach Owlhorn until darkness. His eyes swept the gray twisting road ahead, studying the tawny creases of the surrounding hillslopes with eyes alert for trouble sign. This was Ringbone country and until it was behind him he would not feel otherwise.

"The sodbusters must know they'll have to fight to hold their new homes until law and order comes in," the man said carefully. "Cattlemen know that every quarter section of valley bottom that's fenced in brings the day closer when they'll find themselves pushed back into these desert hills. Any homesteader who isn't a blind fool has surely taken that into account before coming here."

He felt a rising hostility in the girl's sideward glance.

"You're a cowman," she said accusatively. "I saw you leaving Jubal Buckring's ranch. Are you one of the riders who will help terrorize those innocent women and children in the valley?"

He returned her look thoughtfully, feeling the pressure of restrictions which hemmed in his every word, his every act, knowing the impossibility of telling this girl the things she wanted to hear from him.

"The land office opens in four days," he said. "I do not expect to be in this country the day after that. Does that sound like I've joined Buckring?"

Something like relief touched the girl's face as they reined up to let their horses blow at the top of the last ridge overlooking Owlhorn Valley and the green trace of Rawhide Creek.

In the distance they could see the glimmer of sunshine on the white hoods of the homesteaders' wagons, the silver sparkle of the shallow river, and the haze of dust and smoke which obscured the ugly aspects of Owlhorn.

"You are a person of strange contradictions, Cleve Logan," she said. "On the *Sacajawea* I took you to be a man in a hurry to get somewhere and that was what impelled me to help you when your lasso missed its mark. I could not bear to see you miss that boat because of Rossiter's nasty temper. When you met the Klickitat stage yesterday I was glad to see you, glad that Owlhorn was your destination as well as mine. Now you say you are leaving it behind. Doesn't the other side of the hill ever bore you, Cleve?"

He filled and lit his pipe, a habit of his to cover up his thoughts, and sat with one knee hooked over the saddle horn, the sun's bright flash on the backstrap of his gun drawing the girl's eye toward that weapon.

"Do I flatter myself that you'd be sorry to see me head over the hill, Alva?"

The question, bluntly phrased, brought the color to the girl's cheeks.

"If—if you mistook my interest for cheap flirtation,

Cleve, that would make me sorry."

He divined a certain pathos back of her statement and he permitted himself a careful comment. "You're young and uncommonly pretty for a frontier woman, Alva. Back along the trail you've probably had many a man wanting to marry you. What holds you back?"

She sat her saddle stiffly, staring straight ahead.

"A man hurt you some time, some place?" he pressed her, circling the edges of her reserve.

Her voice came softly, "I have never been in love, if that's what you mean. I—I can't allow myself to be."

The fragrance of his tobacco wafted to her and he knew that his nearness touched her, knew that behind her defensive front this girl was capable of deep emotions.

"I think I know," he said. "Your brother. May I ask what caused his affliction? Was he born blind?"

She shook her head. "No. It happened when I was a baby. Dad was a circuit rider in the Alder Gulch mines in Montana, during the rush of '67. One night a pair of claim jumpers shot Dad and ransacked our cabin, hunting for gold dust. They thought Dad was a prospector. When they couldn't find as much as a nugget, they set fire to the cabin."

Alva sucked a deep breath into her lungs, her eyes hardening under the pressure of old memories, long covered up.

"Jeb was a boy of eight then. He came back from town and found the cabin in flames. He went inside, wrapped my crib blanket about me and got me out somehow. But the flames disfigured his face and destroyed his eyesight. Since then I have been the only eyes Jeb has had."

She shook herself out of her mood and managed a smile as they resumed their ride out of the foothills.

"That was twenty years ago," she said. "Jeb educated himself at a seminary and was ordained only this spring in Lewiston. This Owlhorn church is his first parish. We were lucky to find a board of deacons who would hire a blind minister."

They talked of other things during the last lap of their ride along the Rawhide. Not until they were nearing the outermost of the homesteaders' camps along the river east of Owlhorn did Alva Ames comment on the land rush.

"You met this man Duke Perris on the *Sacajawea*," she said. "What do you make of him, Cleve?"

"What do you mean?"

She shrugged, a frown cutting the smooth surface of her brow. "Well, so many of these homesteaders are flocking to that land office of his, Cleve, turning over their precious savings to buy lots which Perris is selling in Owlhorn. I don't like it. He's telling them that in ten years Owlhorn will be the metropolis of the Territory, more important than Seattle or Spokane. That isn't true. Owlhorn will never be anything more than a dot on the map."

Logan was non-committal. "Perhaps the homesteaders are afraid there won't be enough donation claims to go around, the way families are flocking in. Maybe they'd rather speculate with town lots from Perris & Company than be left with nothing."

Circling the south edge of the town they rode directly to the church and dismounted. The vestibule doors were hooked back to ventilate the building and inside they had a glimpse of Jebediah Ames, busy dusting off the worn pews.

"Jeb's so very happy, knowing he will pull his own weight from now on," Alva mused, her eyes moist. "All these years he has felt dependent on me for so much. It isn't a good thing for a man to be a prisoner, Cleve, not even to a sister who loves him more dearly than anything else on earth."

Logan put a hand on the girl's shoulder, feeling the urgency of his own emotions.

"Jeb's obligation to you is no less important to him than yours is to the brother who saved your life in infancy," he said gently. "I'd like to be around when he releases you to pursue your own happiness, Alva. The man who catches your eye will be rich beyond measure, believe me."

He stepped back into stirrups and, the spell broken between them, a harsh note entered his voice as he prepared to ride out of the churchyard.

"I want you to promise me on your honor that you'll take no more joy rides alone on Ringbone range, Alva. This country isn't tame enough for that yet."

Standing on the church steps, Alva Ames solemnly lifted her right hand.

"I promise," she laughed. "No more rides alone."

He put his horse down the hill then, his destination the livery back of the Pioneer House. This ride out from Ringbone had, for the time being, crowded his own tangled destiny out of his head; but he knew it was imperative that he break the news of Toke Grossett's death to Perris before some rider from Buckring's ranch beat him to it.

Later, from the window of his bedroom, he saw the impossibility of contacting Perris in his land office. The place was crowded with homesteaders, as Alva had said, eager to spend their scanty funds for Owlhorn building sites.

He waited until darkness had come again to the valley before going downstairs to eat supper. He saw the lights blossom in the Palace Casino, and the windows of Perris' office go dark.

His meal finished, Logan walked into the darkness of a moonless night, crossing the street to the Palace. At the moment of his entrance through the batwings, the packed house was relatively hushed, listening to Opal Waymire sing a bawdy song to the accompaniment of a Negro pianist.

She was dressed in a low cut scarlet gown ablaze with sequins. Her voice had a throaty, sexual quality which was surprisingly good for a honkytonk singer. During the storm of applause and boot-stomping which followed her number, Logan moved through the crowded place and satisfied himself that Duke Perris was not in the barroom.

Opal caught his eye and he could not mistake the invitation in her motion toward the door of her private office. He shook his head, sending his regrets across that smoke-fouled room, and pushed out through the slatted half-door into the night.

The girl's voice was lifted in another plaintive melody when he reached the alley which separated the Palace from Duke Perris' land office. The front of that building was dark but pinholes of light streamed through the green shades of windows in the back of the building where Perris had his living quarters.

Logan moved down the alley and rounded the corner just as the back door opened to throw its spreading glare of lamplight across the weeds of the back lot.

A pompous-looking man with turkey-wattle jowls and a corpulent figure clad in a long-skirted clawhammer coat stepped out of Perris' room, his profile turned to Logan as he faded back into the deep shadow alongside the clapboard wall.

"You sure this thing is foolproof, Duke?" the fat man spoke timorously around one of Perris' expensive cheroots. "A man in my official position, you know—subject to Federal investigation—it behooves me to watch my step."

Perris' deep voice reassured his visitor from the doorway, out of Logan's sight. "With Stagman disposed of we can't miss, Gulberg. You have the papers ready tomorrow night and I'll have the buyers lined up. I wish you'd change your mind and handle this out at Buckring's place."

Gulberg shook his triple chins in hearty negation.

"Every move I make is watched by these nesters, you understand. To be seen heading toward Ringbone would prejudice my security. Good night, my friend."

The door closed and in the following blackness

Logan heard Gulberg grope his way through the shadows within inches of where Logan stood. The fat man smelled of pomade and cheap whiskey and his breath wheezed asthmatically as he cut up the alley flanking the Palace.

"That'll be Gus Gulberg," ran the thought through Logan's head. "For a Federal land agent in charge of homesteads, Mister Gulberg is keeping strange company tonight."

Logan waited for five minutes before he stepped up on the porch and rattled Perris' doorknob surreptitiously. A moment later the door opened a crack and revealed the promoter's head.

"Oh, Logan," Perris said gruffly. Then, his voice taking on an edge of quick anger, "What are you doing in town? Didn't I give you explicit orders to remain at Buckring's till I sent for you?"

Before Logan could answer Perris blew out his wall lamp and Logan heard the door hinges squeak as Perris joined him on the tiny stoop.

"I had to leave Ringbone in a hurry," Logan drawled.

Perris sucked in a breath. "Why? Sheriff trail you out there?"

Logan laughed softly. "Nothing that simple. Grossett and Buckring sucked me into a trap and threw their guns on me. Seems they got the idea I could turn over a $50,000 Wells-Fargo cache to them. Without your knowledge, by the way."

Perris digested Logan's report at considerable length.

"I'm riding out to Ringbone tonight, Cleve. I'll rake Grossett over the coals for you. I ordered him to lay off you."

Logan laughed again. "That won't be necessary, Perris. I left Grossett with a chunk of lead in his noggin. And Buckring asleep with a sore head. I'm here to see how this affects our deal."

In the darkness Logan kept his hand on gun butt, not being sure of how Perris would take the news of his lieutenant's death. After a moment he heard Perris release a whistling breath.

"Meet me on the outskirts of town in ten minutes," Perris said. "If Buckring's story jibes with yours, we'll write off Grossett as a good riddance. Bounty hunters usually get tangled in their own rope."

Logan stepped noiselessly off the porch, his exact position thereby concealed from the promoter. His whisper came as deadly as a snake's hiss from the darkness. "Perris, if you got any notions about riding out of town with me and pulling a double-cross to square up for Grossett—"

Perris answered quickly, urgently, "No, Logan. Damn it, I trust you. I've got to. It's just that I'm riding out to Ringbone myself—and I want to keep you away from Owlhorn until I send word that John Stagman has arrived."

12: "I AIN'T A GHOST"

Twice on the eight mile ride to the Hole-in-the-Wall, invisible sentinels challenged Cleve Logan and Duke

Perris from coverts in the roadside's darkness.

Buckring, starting tonight, had put a double cordon of guards along the boundary of his ranch abutting the former Indian lands which would be flung open to public settlement. These guards, Logan surmised, had their orders to warn off any homesteader who had ideas of staking out his claim in advance of Gus Gulberg's official opening of the land office.

The alacrity with which the Ringbone sentries granted Perris safe passage behind this curtain of waiting guns gave Logan fresh proof of the authority Duke Perris wielded over Ringbone, pointed up the speculator's mysterious reasons for being in this country.

The surreptitious way Perris had smuggled nearly thirty accomplices to the Horse Heaven country, his vague references to a big deal with Jubal Buckring—these things obviously went beyond any mere sales promotion campaign for building sites in Owlhorn proper. Perris was playing for high stakes, stakes important enough to call for the murder of the Federal lawman who would be assigned to keep law and order in Owlhorn when the land rush opened. Logan had a hunch that this ride to Ringbone tonight would prove the key to the mysterious and sinister undercover doings beyond these brooding hills, something which would affect the destinies of every man, woman and child in Owlhorn Valley for generations to come.

Ranch lights formed their sporadic pattern down in the sooty Hole-in-the-Wall where Ringbone's citadel crouched like a spider at the hub of its web. Perris sent his halloo running ahead as they came within Winchester range of the ranch buildings, and the drum roll of their mounts' hoofs set up the inevitable clamor of barking dogs which in turn started coyotes baying in the remoter hills like echoes.

Perris pulled over to the bunkhouse where his Idaho henchmen were being kept under cover. His shout brought old Pegleg Cochran to the door. Beyond the oldster Logan had a view of the interminable poker games still in progress.

"All the men here, Cochran?" Perris demanded. "Good. Break up those games and have the tables cleared off. Tell the others I'm laying my cards on the table tonight. You'll find out what you were brought over here to accomplish."

Cochran's respectful, "Us-uns was gittin' all-powerful curious tuh see yore hole card, Mister Perris," followed the two riders as they rode on down the poplar-bordered lane toward the lighted windows of the ranch house.

Jubal Buckring's big shape appeared briefly in the open doorway as Perris and Logan reined up at the picket gate. The lamplight put a halo on his white hair, showed the bandage around his skull and the white gleam of a patch of plaster on his nose. He held a lever-action carbine in his hands.

"Jube, I've got Cleve Logan with me," Perris warned the big rancher. "Put down that .30-30 and come out here."

Buckring, one of the most powerful men in the Territory, and whose word was absolute law on the Ringbone, leaned his rifle against the wall and hastened down the gravel path as if he were Perris' slave.

"You know Toke Grossett's lyin' dead out in my feed shed?" Buckring demanded as he reached the gate.

"I know all about that," Duke Perris snapped. "What beats me, Jube, is why you stooped to play for a penny-ante side bet when we've got sky-high stakes in the main pot."

Buckring shifted uneasily before the speculator's anger, completely dominated by the overwhelming personality facing him.

"I thought the gold was worth going after," Buckring mumbled. "My cut of the deal would have helped pay you off, Duke."

Perris spat out an oath. "Logan's job is to handle that U. S. Marshal, which makes him a damn sight more valuable to you than any Wells-Fargo box he may have hid. How far do you think we would get with this land-grab if John Stagman was sitting by Gus Gulberg's elbow when the land office opens?"

The Ringbone boss made a gesture of surrender.

"All right, Duke. Call off your dogs. I've got men who could have handled Stagman as well as Logan here, but that's water over the dam."

Perris motioned for Logan to dismount.

"Let's get over to the bunkhouse," he said, hitching his own horse to the picket fence alongside Logan's dun. "Everything's shaping up okay, Jube. I sealed our bargain with Gulberg tonight. He agreed to everything except coming out here to your place. So far as I can see nothing stands between Ringbone and your toe-hold along the Rawhide."

Cleve Logan walked behind the two conspirators as they headed toward the lighted soddy. Suspense put its electric tingle through every fiber of Logan's being as he gave his sharpest attention to the cryptic remarks Perris was making.

He knew with a keen prescience that tonight would see Perris exposing his hole card for the first time. The men whom Perris had gathered together over two hundred miles from Lewiston's saloons and gambling dives were mere pawns in whatever game Perris and Buckring were playing. This bunkhouse conference would see the ringleaders make their first move of that game, probably the result of months of secret scheming.

The bunkhouse was oppressive with the mingled stench of sweat and tobacco smoke and whiskey reek. The collection of riffraff had cleared off their poker tables in the middle of the room and had banked themselves in tiers along the double-decked sleeping bunks.

Logan moved unobtrusively to the shadows behind the rusty Franklin stove as he saw Pegleg Cochran draw up barrel chairs for Perris and Buckring. From his pocket Perris drew out a bundle which, when unfolded, proved to be a large blueprint of the Horse Heaven Hills and the valley of the Rawhide. The portion of country coming under the provisions of the new Homestead Law had been outlined in red, marked in quarter sections like a big checkerboard. That land,

Logan noticed, was roughly bisected by the meandering course of the Rawhide.

"All right, men," Perris said briskly, pausing to light up a cigar. "Up to now you've been kept in ignorance as to why I brought you here, promising you $200 cash and return boat tickets to Lewiston. The work you'll do to earn your pay is simple, but Mr. Buckring and I can afford no slipups. Any man who wants to back out of this deal, sing out now."

Logan's glance flicked around the half-circle. He saw suspense on some faces, curiosity on others; but the intellectual plane of these men was scaled down to the level of dumb brutes. The promise of Perris' gold was the cement which bonded these derelicts together, the only hold Perris had on their loyalty.

"All right," Perris went on, weighting down the corners of the map. "This paper is a government survey of the portions of the Yakima Indian Reservation which are to be opened as public domain at eight o'clock Monday morning."

The bearded faces bent forward, beady eyes watching the movements of Perris' forefinger with a stolid attention, like children over their depth in a schoolroom discussion.

"The basic idea is this," Perris went on. "If this strip of homesteadable land between Buckring's north fence and the Rawhide River falls into the hands of homesteaders, it means Ringbone is cut off forever from its source of water and from access to the Indian land it leases for summer graze across the river. Each of these squares represents one section of land, one square mile. Each section comprises four homesteads. You can all see Mr. Buckring's desire to get title to an unbroken strip of land fronting the river for approximately fifteen miles east of Owlhorn, that being Ringbone's dimension."

Cleve Logan felt the hard thump of his heart jarring him to his bootheels. Perris had lifted a corner of the veil now, but his words so far meant little to the minds of his audience.

But Logan grasped the full significance of this monstrous thing Perris was engineering. It was to be a land grab on a scale without precedent in Washington Territory, a wholesale theft of public land which would accrue to Ringbone's profit at the expense of uncounted homesteaders now waiting innocently at Owlhorn for the land office to give them their chance at future homesites.

"I'm just an ignorant boozehound, Mister Perris," spoke up the one-legged Cochran. "But I don't savvy where me an' the boys you hired in Lewiston fit in on this deal. You didn't fetch us over here to make homesteaders out of us, did yuh?"

Perris flicked ash from his cheroot, sizing up his audience to make sure they had their thorough attention on what he was about to tell them.

"I'm coming to that, Cochran. Tomorrow night, Mr. Buckring will escort you men to Owlhorn under cover of darkness. We will meet in the back of the Palace Casino, where the government land agent will be on hand with the necessary legal documents to file homestead claims on thirty quarter sections facing the Rawhide."

Perris jabbed a forefinger on his map.

"Each of these river front homesteads is numbered," he went on. "I'm assigning a numbered quarter section to each of you. All you've got to do is memorize that number so that when Gulberg calls your number, you can step forward and sign the papers he will provide."

Logan mopped the moisture from his brow. The deal was clear enough for even these simpletons to understand. Perris had imported dummy homesteaders to lay claim to contiguous land forming a fifteen mile long strip between Ringbone's north fence and the Rawhide River. The choicest land in Owlhorn Valley would thus pass under Jubal Buckring's indirect control.

"Hold on a second," put in Pegleg Cochran. "I don't know shucks about law, but when you file on a homestead you got to prove up on yore claim for a year afore you git title, don't you? Speakin' for myself, I don't cotton to spend a hull year bustin' sod, not at my age."

Jubal Buckring entered the discussion for the first time. The rancher's patience with these simpletons was wearing thin, and when he spoke it was with a waspish anger.

"As soon as you numbskulls get your John Henry on Gulberg's papers you'll be comin' back here," Buckring explained. "You'll head back to the Columbia River with the steamer tickets Perris will give you tomorrow night and go back where you came from.

You'll collect the rest of your pay from Perris' agent in Lewiston. That's all you got to do."

Cochran stroked his carrot-colored beard nervously.

"You'll git the papers, Mister Buckring," the oldster said, "but it seems to me that the law will ketch up with us an' want to find out why we ain't livin' on our homesteads."

Perris stood up, waving Cochran into silence.

"All details have been attended to and are none of your concern, Pegleg!" he snapped. "The law doesn't know any of you from Adam, which is why I went out of the Territory to round you up. Mr. Buckring will have his own men to throw up shacks and make a pretense of proving up on those thirty homesteads. The papers will be predated by Mr. Gulberg at the land office, and if anybody investigates, Gulberg will swear you men were the first in line when the land rush opened Monday."

Cleve Logan's brain was swirling as he listened to Perris assigning homestead numbers to each man in the bunkhouse, at the same time jotting that man's name on his map.

Bits of this jigsaw puzzle were falling into shape now. Tomorrow night was three days in advance of the official opening of the land office. Gus Gulberg, no doubt, had pocketed a fat bribe from Perris in return for his cooperation in this legal skullduggery. He hesitated to guess what price Jubal Buckring was paying Perris for accomplishing this land grab. The sum would probably run into six figures. Buckring's price for saving Ringbone's future. With the waterfront

132

boundary sewed up in the name of dummy home-steaders in Buckring's employ, the cattle king's position in these hills would be impregnable.

Behind the steady drone of voices in the stuffy bunkhouse, Logan was thinking of the homesteader families camped down on the outskirts of Owlhorn tonight, ignorant of this theft of land. He thought of Tex Kinevan, who had his eye on one of those very river front quarter sections which Gus Gulberg would prematurely record in the name of one of Perris' fake claimants.

Only one man stood between Ringbone's illegal seizure of the river front strip—United States Marshal John Stagman. That obstacle Perris had guaranteed to pay $5,000 to remove.

Rolling up the map, the conference finished, Perris stepped over to where Cleve Logan stood behind the stove.

"You'll keep under cover here on the ranch," Perris said. "Buckring won't bother you. I believe you understand now why it is so important that Stagman's murder cannot be traced to my organization or to any Ringbone rider."

Half an hour later Duke Perris rode out of the Hole-in-the-Wall. Reaching Owlhorn, the promoter stabled his horse and then made his way to Opal Waymire's saloon, admitting himself to the girl's private office in the rear of the building by means of his duplicate key.

He was startled to find Opal Waymire seated on a divan there with a gorilla-built man in a plucked beaver coat and a brand new hat of the Mormon variety. The man's right arm reclined in a dirty flour-sack sling, splinted from elbow to wrist.

For a moment, Perris stood staring at the ruffian Opal was entertaining, his eyes wide in disbelief. Finally he choked out in a hoarse whisper, "*Blackie Marengo!* I thought you drowned in the Columbia."

Marengo's features wrinkled in a grin.

"I ain't no ghost, boss. I would 'a' drowned, ifn a digger Indian hadn't hauled me into his dugout, right after I fell off o' the boat. It taken me this long to git here. Hoofed it as far as Winegarten's wood camp an' stole myself a hoss there."

Perris continued to stare at Marengo as if he were seeing an apparition. In the background Opal Waymire was standing motionless, her face marble white, her eyes haunted, terror-stricken.

"Duke," she said, "Blackie has terrible news."

"What's up?" Perris demanded. "What news?"

Marengo poured himself a generous shot of bourbon from a bottle on Opal's table.

"Your gal friend tells me," Marengo said smugly, "that Cleve Logan is a convict I run into at Deer Lodge. Well, it was Cleve Logan who busted my wing an' chucked me into the river the other night. I ran into him after Grossett told me to go to your cabin."

Perris clutched a chair back for support. "Trig Fetterman threw you overboard? Why?"

Marengo's countenance twisted sardonically.

"Trig Fetterman, hell! Cleve Logan is the man who put me in the penitentiary for rustlin' cattle, boss. He

ain't no more Trig Fetterman than I am. He wears
John Stagman's collar, always has. Cleve Logan is a
deputy United States marshal!"

13: TRAP FOR A LAWMAN

The room wheeled dizzily around Duke Perris, a
blur in which the white face of Opal Waymire and the
anvil-jawed visage of Blackie Marengo alone stood
out in sharp focus.

It was the first time in the better than ten years that
Opal had known this cold-blooded man that she had
ever seen anything jar loose his iron grip on his
reflexes. As Perris sagged onto the divan, the girl
jerked the whiskey bottle out of Marengo's fist and
poured Perris a stiff drink.

"Here," she whispered, thrusting the glass into
Perris' shaking hand. "We've let a John Law spy slip
into our own camp, Duke. What are we going to do?"

Perris downed the stinging liquor at a gulp, felt its
heat put a grip on his nerves.

"Cleve Logan wears a star," he muttered thickly.
"Are you certain of that, Blackie?"

Marengo settled himself on the sofa. His face wore
a complacent grin.

"Certain? Hell, yes. Ain't I just told you he was the
deputy who sent me to the rockpile? Last time I seen
Cleve Logan was in the warden's office when I was
swappin' my name for a number. I told Logan then I'd
kill him next time our trails crossed. And I put my
mark on his hide the other night on the boat. Logan

was John Stagman's right-hand man over in Wyoming for years. I'm telling you straight, boss."

Perris put his elbows on his knees and covered his face with his hands, his brain still stunned by the impact of Marengo's bombshell and its unprobed ramifications.

"If only Blackie had been on deck when Cleve Logan made that play at Riverbend," Opal Waymire's voice came as if from a remote distance from Perris' ears. "His trickery is easy to figure out now, Duke. Logan put himself in your eye with such a melodramatic scene that you swallowed the bait—leaving his horse on the dock and throwing a lariat to stop the boat. And John Stagman showing up with a posse five minutes later. Anyone would have thought Logan was a desperado on the run. The whole thing was deliberately staged."

When Perris lifted his face from his hands he had regained his old composure.

"Sure," he laughed bitterly. "Sure. Hindsight is great stuff. Stagman must have got wind of my going over to Lewiston and chartering the *Sacajawea* to haul those dummy homesteaders back here. Stagman must have put this Cleve Logan on my trail because Logan could pass himself off for Trig Fetterman."

Opal's face was a hard mask, harsh lines of strain robbing her of her natural beauty.

"Well, the trick worked," she said. "Logan convinced us he was an escaped convict with a price on his head. I shudder to think what would have happened if Blackie Marengo hadn't turned up."

Marengo poured himself another drink, enjoying his position as an equal of these two.

"I knew Fetterman at Deer Lodge pen," he said thickly. "He's the same height an' complexion as Logan, but otherwise they're completely different men. Why, hell, the grapevine at the pen claimed that Cleve Logan turned in his badge after he nailed me and bought hisself a little ranch over in the Blue Mountains. I figger John Stagman must have hauled Logan out of retirement just to find out what you were up to in Owlhorn, boss."

Perris got to his feet, his hand going up to the gold bullet ornament on his watch chain. Opal, watching that oft-repeated mannerism of Perris', found herself pondering on how apt that luck charm was. A golden bullet symbolizing the forces that ruled Perris' life—riches and violence, gold and gunsmoke.

"I've got to think this thing out. No time to foul my head with alcohol," Perris said, waving aside another offered drink. "A deputy marshal spying in my own camp. I can't believe I could have been duped so completely."

He looked up, remembering something. "Opal, Logan sat in on my powwow with the dummy homesteaders over at the Ringbone tonight. He knows our whole setup from A to Z. Right this minute he's probably making his plans to arrest Gus Gulberg and the rest of us when we meet in town tomorrow night."

Opal Waymire's painted mouth made an inverted scarlet crescent against the chalky pallor of her face. Suddenly, and without apparent cause, she began to

137

laugh hysterically, her arms folded across her breast, tears running down her cheeks.

"What's so damned funny?" demanded Perris.

The girl got herself under control. "John Stagman's been trying to pin something on you for fifteen years, Duke," she said. "Up to now you've been too slippery for the law. This time he almost got the goods on you. A conviction for this land grab would put you and Jube Buckring behind bars for twenty years."

Perris saw the macabre humor in the situation, for a hint of a smile touched the corners of his predatory lips.

"Sure, laugh at me, kid. I hired Stagman's own deputy to bushwhack Stagman. Go ahead. Laugh."

Blackie Marengo, well on his way toward a king-sized drunk, turned to Opal and dropped a hand on her thigh.

"Looks like l'il ol' Blackie saved your bacon, gal. Mebbe from here on out you won't be so uppity with ol' Blackie."

The crack of Perris' palm lashing Marengo's cheek was like a pistol shot in the keyed-up atmosphere of this room.

"Go upstairs and sleep off this bender," Perris raged. "Stay out of sight until I send for you. And the next time you lay a paw on Opal I'll stomp your guts out."

Marengo, shocked cold sober, struggled to his feet and followed Opal over to a side door opening on stairs which led to the percentage girls' rooms upstairs.

When Opal turned to face Duke Perris, the big man

said, "This thing is like a string of firecrackers, honey. Every few seconds another one explodes in my ear. Just this morning Tex Kinevan rode out to Ringbone and tipped off Grossett that Logan was really Trig Fetterman. That means Kinevan's in on this deal with Logan too!"

The girl put a white arm around the promoter's shoulders.

"We've got to get out of here tonight," she said. "Kinevan is probably a deputy marshal too. We're in this too deep to buck the Federals, Duke. Let's pack up now!"

Perris shrugged off the girl's embrace.

"No. No," he said. "We still got time enough to swing this deal. We've got to collect our money from Buckring before John Stagman shows up. By the time Buckring gets wise, we'll be a long way from Owlhorn, sweetheart."

Opal Waymire walked over to the door which opened on the crowded barroom, and left the room. A few moments later she returned, her cheeks still chalk-white under her rouge.

"Tex Kinevan's shooting pool in the back room," she reported. "If you want, I could get him in here for you."

After a long pause, Perris came to a decision.

"No," he vetoed her idea. "Taking Kinevan tonight might tip off my hand, and give Cleve Logan his chance to fly the coop. Do you think Kinevan saw Blackie Marengo tonight?"

"No, Duke. Marengo only reached Owlhorn shortly before you got back from Ringbone. He came directly to the Palace. Kinevan's been shooting pool since suppertime."

Some of the tension left Perris' face.

"That's good. Kinevan must have known the real facts behind Blackie's disappearing off the *Sacajawea* the other night. Funny, I passed it off as an accident, a result of that railing caving in. Lord, what if Marengo had drowned? What if that Indian hadn't fished him out of the river?"

Opal shrugged her powdered shoulders.

"You'd have found yourself looking into Logan's gun. And has it occurred to you that the local sheriff must be in on this scheme of John Stagman's?"

Perris gave this possibility a moment's thought.

"Another firecracker in the string," he said. "Sure, I imagine old Farnick knows Logan is a Federal deputy."

Opal Waymire crossed the room and flung her arms around Perris, kissing him passionately.

"I'm afraid, Duke," she pleaded. "We've got to get out of town while we can. Drop everything we've built up and leave Owlhorn forever. Logan is too dangerous for us to handle. You ought to know just how dangerous he really is, darling."

But Perris' jaw was set in a dogged outthrust.

"This land grab is worth one hundred thousand dollars to us, Opal. Buckring's got the money in his safe. It's the biggest deal of my lifetime. We've put a year into planning this thing. I hate to be run out of the game while I'm holding all the aces."

Opal laughed bitterly. "Cleve Logan has a pat hand."

"But I've seen his hole card, thanks to Marengo's tip-off. Who are we bucking? Logan and Tex Kinevan. And John Stagman, who isn't due to show up until Saturday or Sunday. We can rake in this jackpot tomorrow night, Opal."

Knowing this man as she did, knowing the stark courage which complemented Perris' criminal mentality, Opal Waymire knew the futility of urging Perris to drop the gamble he faced here, in favor of the safe way out.

Slumping down on the sofa, the girl asked bleakly, her face shining with cold perspiration in the lamplight, "What will you do?"

Perris wheeled to face her, all his old aplomb showing in his eyes.

"Logan can be brought in with Buckring and the Lewiston boys tomorrow night," he said. "We'll make certain Tex Kinevan is on hand as well. You'll take their guns at the door, Opal. That's the sheriff's rule, and will arouse no suspicion on their part. You'll reserve the poolroom for our use tomorrow night. That poolroom will be my trap for Logan and Kinevan."

Having made his plan, Perris leaned down and kissed the girl. Then he let himself out through the back entrance and Opal Waymire, stepping to the alley window a moment later, peeped through the shutters to see a light go on in Perris' living quarters behind the land office next door.

Thinking over Duke Perris' decision, Opal Waymire was struck by what she believed was an unnecessary angle—getting his revenge on Cleve Logan and Tex

141

Kinevan before going ahead with his conspiracy with Gus Gulberg and, in turn, receiving Jubal Buckring's $100,000 pay-off.

The logical and less hazardous alternative would be to keep Logan waiting out at the Ringbone, complete the deal with Gulberg without drawing Tex Kinevan into the picture at all, and making a secret exit from Owlhorn, leaving Buckring to hold the bag when Logan made his official report to U. S. Marshal Stagman.

But that was contrary to the harsh forces which governed Perris' character. To Perris, retribution against Logan and Kinevan was as important as the land grab scheme which had brought them to Owlhorn in the first place.

Nearly an hour later Opal Waymire left the Palace. The feverish activity on Owlhorn's main street did not cease at sundown; carpenters were busy throwing up saloons and store buildings by the glare of flaming tar barrels.

Shielding herself against the chill of the river fog with a shawl, Opal made her way up the hill to Alva Ames' home in the Methodist parsonage. A light still gleamed from the front windows, though the hour was past midnight.

Avoiding the long shaft of light from the Ames' window, Opal approached the parsonage. She saw Alva seated at a table writing. Her blind brother was nowhere in sight, and Opal concluded that Jebediah Ames had retired for the night.

Alva came to the door in response to Opal's knock.

Surprise was limned in the girl's features as she recognized the owner of the notorious Palace Casino at the doorstep, the tight-pulled folds of her shawl accentuating the brassy hue of her bleached hair.

"I beg your pardon for this intrusion," Opal whispered. "I can't come in. But I must see you."

"Of course, Miss Waymire," Alva said, stepping outside and easing the door shut behind her. "Are you in trouble?"

The honkytonk singer's fingers were like ice as they gripped Alva's wrist.

"It's about Cleve Logan," she whispered, an almost irrational note entering her voice. "He's in terrible danger. I want you to ride out to Ringbone in the morning and deliver a message to him."

Alva drew in a breath, remembering her solemn pledge to Cleve never to ride across Ringbone's boundaries again without proper escort.

"If—if it is really important," she faltered, "I will do as you say, Miss Waymire."

A sob put its tremolo in Opal's voice.

"Just—just tell Cleve that Duke Perris knows he is a deputy United States marshal, Alva. Cleve will understand."

With which Opal Waymire released Alva's hand and turned to vanish in the darkness.

For a long time Alva Ames stood in the starlight by the parsonage door, giving way to the full run of her unleashed emotions. Cleve Logan a deputy marshal!

The corpse of Toke Grossett was consigned to an unmarked grave in a coulee overlooking the Ringbone headquarters just as the morrowing sun lifted over the bald tangents of the Horse Heaven Hills and poured its bursting golden flood into Buckring's Hole-in-the-Wall.

Cleve Logan saw the bounty hunter's tarp-shrouded body leave on its one way trip by buckboard wagon, as he was heading for the cookshack and breakfast, with one of Buckring's roustabouts acting as grave-digger.

The new day found Logan's nerves eating at him. Joining the poker games with Perris' unkempt henchmen at the bunkhouse had no appeal for him. He was keyed up with a sense of climax rushing toward him, knowing that tonight marked showdown, the closing phase of the assignment which had brought him out of retirement at the request of his old friend and superior, John Stagman.

Going to the harness shop where he could sort out his thoughts in seclusion, Logan settled down to kill time soaping his saddle gear.

One thing was clear—the time was past due for a conference with Sheriff Vick Farnick in Owlhorn. But getting off the heavily guarded ranch when he was under strict orders from Perris to lie low until sent for might make a trip to town well nigh impossible.

He was debating whether to saddle up and attempt

to bluff his way through the gantlet of Buckring's guards along the Owlhorn road when the shot sent its flat echoes breaching the early morning quiet.

The slam and crash of that gun's report volleyed interminably off the shoulders of the Hole-in-the-Wall, and brought Jubal Buckring out on his front porch to scan the horizon with his field glasses.

Ringbone was as edgy as a rattler in dog-days, jumpy from long built-up tensions. During the night the roundup crews had returned to the Hole; like an army massing for an attack, they were down at the main bunkhouse oiling their guns and readying their riding gear.

For his part, Logan dismissed the shot as some outrider knocking off a rattlesnake or a skulking coyote. He had resumed his work in the archway of the harness shop when his ears caught a drum roll of hoofs and a Ringbone rider appeared on the summit road. A wind off the outer valley rolled a great streamer of gritty volcanic dust off the ridge which led to the lone pine and proved that the horseman had come out of the hills from a right angle.

Logan put his sharpened interest on the approaching rider, who lashed his horse up the poplar-bordered lane at a full gallop and hammered past the outbuildings to rein up in front of Buckring's gate.

Buckring was on hand to greet his scout, the field glasses slung about his neck. Fifty yards away, Cleve Logan caught the cattle king's anxious question.

"What was that shootin', Buck? Homesteader squattin' along our fence?"

Buck's answer was pitched in a voice which showed the strain of an all-night patrol, "Funny thing, Jube. Couple of hours before sunup, a rider tried to sneak past Lon Kirkman at the end of the section line road. Turned out to be a girl from town. Claimed she was the new skypilot's sister."

Cleve Logan shared Buckring's astonishment.

"Why should Alva Ames be ridin' the hill road before daylight? Kirkman find out?"

"No," Buck drawled, "Lon told her nobody was ridin' to the Hole-in-the-Wall an' she turned back toward town. Then just a few minutes ago, I was cookin' myself a snack of bait up on the rocky patch—"

Buck paused to light up a brown paper cigarette which he had been rolling, and the interruption put an edge of suspense against Logan.

"Fixin' breakfast," Buck went on, "I heard somethin' or somebody pushin' a hoss through jackrabbit Coulee. I had myself a look. It was this same girl, tryin' to sneak into the Hole from the west. She'd dodged the lookouts on the ridge an' was almost in sight of the Hole here."

Remembering the gunshot, Cleve Logan felt a shock of apprehension stir the hairs on his neck. Buckring had the same reaction, for his question cut sharp and clear across the intervening distance. "You shot her, Buck? You killed a woman on my range?"

Buck shook his head.

"I ain't that crazy, boss. But I dropped her pony out from under her when she tried to beat me out of that coulee. Only thing I could do, me bein' afoot. An' you give orders to let no strangers pass."

Buckring's fists shook the picket gate.

"You set the Ames woman afoot inside my range," he said. "I can't very well blame you, Buck, at that. Where is she now?"

Buck picked up his reins and curvetted his lathered pony away from the gate.

"Kirkman was ridin' in an' come over to investigate. The girl acted like a scairt rabbit, wouldn't tell us why she was snoopin' around. So Kirkman give her a stirrup an' right now he's takin' her back to Owlhorn. He'll set her right down on the church steps, you can bank on that."

Buckring returned to the house and Buck headed for the barns, his all-night tour of duty finished.

Worry carved its notch between Logan's brows. Alva Ames had seemingly taken desperate chances in her persistent effort to pierce Ringbone's cordon, failing only when her horse was killed under her. Why?

Instinct, compelling intuition which Logan could not shake off, told him that he was the object of the preacher's sister attempting to reach Hole-in-the-Wall against her pledged oath not to ride on Ringbone range alone.

The feeling persisted, mounting until it was like a tight-coiled metal spring inside him. In the end, Logan knew he could not wait until night to sneak off the ranch and ride to Owlhorn. Alva's frantic attempts to reach Ringbone could not have stemmed from any girlish whim. Alva Ames had not been joy riding last night, as she had been yesterday morning.

Carrying his saddle over to the cavvy corral, Logan roped his dun and was leading it through the gate when Jubal Buckring emerged from the tanks alongside the windmill tower, a drawn Bisley .38 flashing in the sun.

"Ridin' somewhere, Logan?"

Logan took his own good time about answering. This proved he was being watched. Buckring, or one of the ranch crew, had divined his intentions to saddle and ride and had made this quick countermove to thwart him.

"Any objections, Buckring?" Logan asked, sliding his bridle reins through taut fingers.

The Ringbone boss came forward, hefting the Bisley, his thumb holding the weapon at half cock. It was the same .38 that had put Toke Grossett under the sod.

"You're under the same orders as those bums in the bunkhouse yonder," Buckring snapped. "No man leaves this ranch until we ride to Owlhorn tonight in a bunch. And you won't be with us."

Logan pushed the flat of his left palm against his thigh, feeling the hard outline of the ball-pointed star which was pinned to the inside of his overalls just under the waistband.

The words DEPUTY UNITED STATES MARSHAL were etched on that badge. He had only to flash it in Buckring's eyes to call this rancher's bluff.

"No reason why I can't go to town early and wait for the rest of you," he said tentatively. "I'm not a prisoner here. I know enough to steer shy of Perris' office during daylight."

Buckring waggled his gun. "You couldn't get past my road guards anyhow. Turn your bronc back in the corral, Logan. My men got orders to shoot anybody who tries to leave the Hole-in-the-Wall today."

Logan had his bad moment then, rashness crowding his impulses hard. He could turn away, bait Buckring into holstering his gun and then beat him to the draw. He knew that. But such a play would accomplish nothing; it might tear down everything he had risked to build up since accepting John Stagman's suicide assignment to dig into Duke Perris' secret activities.

"You win," Logan said shortly. "I was just getting restless to get that bunkhouse stink out of my nose. It ain't important."

Buckring kept his gun in the open until Logan had turned his dun back into the cavvy. Then Buckring returned to the ranch house and stationed himself on his front porch, where he could command a view of the horse corral and all exits from the Hole.

For Cleve Logan, the remainder of this day dragged on paralyzed feet. The riddle of Alva Ames' motive in making a night ride into these forbidden hills upset the even run of Logan's thinking, hinting as it did of some unforeseen development in Owlhorn that might concern him.

He wondered briefly if John Stagman had arrived ahead of schedule and that she, believing him to be an outlaw on the dodge, might be trying to warn him. But he put that idea aside as improbable; she had given him no cause to believe that she had him ticketed for an owlhoot rider. So far as he knew he had her full trust and faith.

Suspense began to penetrate the stolid ranks of the poker players from Lewiston when, at the conclusion of a hastily devoured supper, Duke Perris showed up at Buckring's gate and went inside to confer with his accomplice.

When full dark had come to the Hole-in-the-Wall, it was not actually sunset time. The Washington sky was prematurely blackened by great racks of dust clouds which presaged a storm roaring in off the Columbia basin desert to the north.

Gusts of wind, forerunners of a tempest, scoured the dusty floor of the cavvy corral when Pegleg Cochran and the other Perris henchmen saddled up for their ride to town and their rendezvous with the speculator's accomplice, U. S. land agent Gus Gulberg.

Logan remained in the bunkhouse, showing no trace of the excitement he felt. He would give Perris and Buckring a ten minute head start before saddling up for his own departure for Owlhorn; the approaching storm would make it easier to cut through the road guards.

With any kind of luck, he could beat the cavalcade to town and tip off Sheriff Farnick that their trap was ready to spring tonight, catching the principals of this land grab plot en masse at the poolroom in the Palace Casino.

The arrival of Duke Perris himself at the bunkhouse, however, brought an unexpected change in his plans.

"Saddle up, Cleve," the promoter ordered. "I'll need you to file on a dummy homestead to fill in for Blackie Marengo, one of my men who disappeared en route."

Logan had no choice but to comply; any hesitance on his part could not be explained. Ten minutes later, joining the nervous group of men out in the lane, Logan made the discovery that this ride to Owlhorn would be under heavy guard.

Buckring had drawn six Ringbone cowpunchers from his crew to box in Perris' fake homesteaders, reminding Logan of a herd of cattle on the trail. For himself, the presence of armed guards would make it difficult to break away from the group even for a few minutes and give him time to enlist Sheriff Farnick's help tonight.

A high wind, filled with abrasive particles of lava dust scoured off the Rattlesnake Hills beyond the Yakima River, stung the faces of the riders as they followed the section line road due north. When Owlhorn's lights appeared through the thickening dust clouds a mile off, Buckring and Perris left the river road and swung along the spurs of the foothills south of the town.

Thus approaching Owlhorn from the rear, Perris gave the order to dismount when they were a city block from the main street and the Palace Casino.

Hitching their mounts to an old-time stake and rider fence which bounded the courthouse square, Perris called the riders into a compact bunch, his Ringbone guards circling them at once.

Slipping out of this group and reaching Farnick's office in the jail was, for the moment, impossible. Logan heard Perris give them their final instructions.

"We'll enter the Palace from the back. Keep quiet and strike no matches. If any of you happen to be totin' guns, you'll surrender them to the house man, that being the local sheriff's orders for anybody entering the city limits. Stick close together and keep quiet. All right, Buckring. Let's go."

Logan felt the weight of the Colt .45 riding his flank and debated whether to discard his gun harness and attempt to hide his six-shooter inside a boot.

He thought, I'm a fool for postponing my talk with Farnick. I didn't expect things to break so soon.

Perris and Buckring were steering for a lighted window in the pool hall annex at the rear of Opal Waymire's gambling dive. Loose cans and bottles rattled underfoot as they shuffled across the vacant lot.

These hoodlums, awed by the secrecy which surrounded their arrival in Owlhorn, were silent as sheep. Circling them, Logan could hear above the storm's approaching violence the jingle of spur chains as Ringbone riders, guns out, stood ready to cut any strays back into the herd.

They reached the black shadows behind the Palace and were shielded there from the blast of the approaching storm. The gale howled in weird banshee tones through loose shingles on Owlhorn's roofs, rattled windows and bent trees like saplings.

Through the window, Cleve Logan saw two men inside, shooting pool. One was the drummer off the

Klickitat stage; the other was Tex Kinevan.

Seeing Kinevan, Logan relaxed. Here was his chance to offset the predicament he found himself in. Once inside, Perris would no doubt order Kinevan and the drummer to leave. A whispered word to Kinevan would tip off Sheriff Vick Farnick that this was the night to strike and nip this land grab plot in the bud.

Perris was met at the rear door by a white-jacketed poolroom attendant, who spoke briefly to the speculator. Logan heard Perris laugh and hand over a six gun to the house man. Jubal Buckring, the next man inside, surrendered his .38 Bisley. Logan saw that Buckring was carrying a carpetbag, and deduced that that bag contained his pay-off for Perris. The floor man made no attempt to search the contents of that bag for concealed weapons.

"Sheriff's orders," the floor man was saying. "Got to enforce his gun-totin' rule or he'd padlock the house. Your guns, gents."

Old Pegleg Cochran, first of the Lewistonians to get in out of the night, surrendered an ancient derringer and received a numbered claim check in return.

Stepping into the yellow glare of the big ceiling lamp, Cleve Logan unbuckled his shell belt and handed it over, pocketing his claim check. Behind him, each of the hoodlums was being deftly frisked for any concealed weapons on his person.

Milling around with the others, Logan worked his way toward the corner table where Kinevan and the fat drummer had stopped their game, puzzled by such an influx of customers through the back door.

Across the room, Perris and Buckring had seated themselves on one of the benches flanking the billiard tables. Gus Gulberg, the Federal land agent who would be the key figure in tonight's conspiracy, was nowhere in the room.

Halting alongside Kinevan, Logan stoked his briar and lifted cupped hands to shield his mouth while lighting up. Around his pipestem he put his urgent whisper to the Texan.

"Tonight's the pay-off. In here. Tell the sheriff."

By no flicker of a facial muscle did Kinevan indicate that any message had reached his ears. He leaned across the pool table to make a shot. Straightening up, he muttered, "Good luck, kid."

Over in the corner by the door, all was confusion as the Lewiston group hunted out seats, plainly showing the nerve strain they were laboring under. The house man, carrying the guns he had collected in a bucket, stepped along the wall to where Kinevan and the drummer were playing and said courteously:

"Have to refund your dimes on the game, gents. The boss has engaged all the tables for a little tournament tonight."

Logan took a cue out of a wall rack and was idly chalking it as he saw Kinevan and the drummer follow the house man toward the barroom entrance. Kinevan, tarrying to rack his cue, found his way blocked by the towering figure of Duke Perris.

Down the length of the crowded room, Cleve Logan heard Perris address the Texas cowboy.

"You needn't leave, friend. This is a sort of reunion

of shipmates off the *Sacajawea*, you might say. I'm putting up a fifty dollar prize to the winner of our little pool tournament. Stick around and join us."

Knots of muscle appeared in the corners of Cleve Logan's cheeks. That's phoney as hell, the wild thought speared through his mind as he saw Kinevan hesitate. Perris is up to something.

"No, thanks, Mister Perris," Kinevan drawled. "I been playin' steady since five o'clock. Aim to get myself a snack of bait and try my luck at rondo-coolo out front. Thanks, anyway."

Beyond them, the house man shut the barroom door, and Logan distinctly heard the click of a bolt in its socket. He thought, We're locked in. The back door was blocked by the tall figure of Jubal Buckring, his pale eyes holding a strange malevolence as they met Logan's.

"Come on, come on, friend Kinevan!" Perris' hearty boom rang out in this confusion. "The only real competition you'll have is when Blackie Marengo gets here. He just got to town. This little party is in Blackie's honor, you might say."

Cleve Logan's glance caught Kinevan's for a panicked interval. Blackie Marengo back in Owlhorn, arisen from a watery grave? Perris might be bluffing, testing the reaction of the two men he had so cleverly disarmed and maneuvered into this trap.

Across half the length of the poolroom, Tex Kinevan's eyes flashed their message of despair to Logan. If Perris spoke truth, neither of them would leave this room alive.

155

"You're staying, Kinevan?" Perris' voice prompted the Texan.

"All right, Perris," Kinevan said, his voice even and casual, betraying none of the deadly tension that rode him in this moment. "I'll challenge you, Cleve Logan. Might as well play out this thing together."

The Lewiston hoodlums, sensing nothing of the drama which this casual crosstalk held, found themselves convenient perches to watch the start of what they seriously supposed to be a pool tournament in the making.

Logan racked the balls, flipped a coin with Kinevan to decide who should break, and had his first try at the cueball.

Making that shot, Logan dropped three balls in the webbed pockets of the table, bringing a hum of approval from the spectators and a soft comment from Duke Perris which removed any shred of doubt as to the death trap they had entered here tonight.

"That was a nice shot, Marshal. Blackie Marengo couldn't have done any better."

15: BEHIND THE 8-BALL

For Logan, the "Trig Fetterman" masquerade was over.

By the use of the single word "Marshal" just now, Duke Perris had dispelled any doubt as to the truth of Blackie Marengo's return from the dead.

Kinevan, hearing Perris' ominous hint, likewise understood. This was a trap, a room they could not hope to leave alive. Their guns, deposited on the backbar rack out front by now, were as inaccessible as the remotest star. The sheriff, unaware of the grim events shaping up in his town tonight, was probably making his first night cruise of the main street deadfalls about now. In any case, he would not penetrate the Palace Casino as far as this locked poolroom.

Kinevan felt a renewed admiration for the big rider he called friend, as he saw Cleve Logan lining up his cue between thumb and curled index finger for another combination shot. By no flick of muscle or change of glance had Logan given any sign of having heard Perris brand him for the incognito lawman he was.

During the time it took Logan to finish a run of three more shots, he had thought out this situation and, like Kinevan across the table, saw no way out of it. He was sure from the stare which Jubal Buckring kept on him, steady as a serpent's, that the Ringbone cattle boss had been warned of his alter ego role, which made a farce of the Wells-Fargo treasure map he had sketched in Buckring's office yesterday.

As for Pegleg Cochran and the other derelicts, Logan knew them to be completely innocent of anything extraordinary in the air tonight. Their reason for being here was obvious to Logan. Perris would continue to goad him with repeated references to Marengo's impending appearance in this room, hoping to bait Logan into attempting some desperation move with a billiard cue or other improvised weapon.

Such an attack would warrant Perris or Buckring to shoot him down in cold blood—Logan was under no illusions as to the fact that the two conspirators carried concealed arms—and the riffraff would make handy witnesses to dispose of any formalities with Sheriff Vick Farnick.

By the same token, neither Perris nor Buckring would be likely to draw a gun and cut either himself or Kinevan down without provocation, before these nerve-taut Idahoans. The immediate course, then, was for the two trapped prisoners to stall along, showing no sign that their nerves were nearing the cracking point under this intolerable and totally hopeless threat of doom.

When it came time for Kinevan to play, the Texan observed gravely, "This table ain't level, kid. We'll switch to the center table and I'll spot you the balls you've already racked up. Fair enough?"

Perris and Buckring, their own faces beginning to show the pressure they were under, exchanged quick glances. Behind Kinevan's innocuous proposal lay a definite purpose, Logan knew—by shifting to the central table they would not only be under the big ceiling lamp, the room's only source of light, but would also be alongside the two windows opening on the side alley.

Kinevan, well aware that his danger was equal to Logan's, was making this bold and desperate bid to give them a fighting chance to attempt a getaway before gunplay broke loose.

While the two pool players were engaged in

changing tables, Duke Perris decided on a change of strategy. Facing his oxlike crew of homestead applicants, he said sharply, "You men get out of here. Buckring, take them into my quarters next door."

Out of his abysmal ignorance of the true state of affairs, old Pegleg Cochran protested querulously, "Ain't we goin' to have a chanct at that fifty dollar prize for the best pool playin', Mister Perris? I'll take on both o' them galoots yonder with one hand tied behind my back an' beat 'em forty ways from the jack—"

Cleve Logan saw the unmistakable relief on Jubal Buckring's face as he unlocked the rear door and stood aside while the men shuffled out into the wind-ripped night. That open door gave them no advantage; bolting through it, jammed as it was, would be inviting disaster.

Perris' motive in emptying the poolroom was not difficult to arrive at. Having given up the idea of forcing his two victims to make the first hostile move, Perris was getting rid of the witnesses to what would soon occur in this room.

"Looks like you're behind the eight-ball, don't it, Marshal?" Perris jeered as the door closed on the last of the toughs. The promoter's left hand was toying with the golden bullet on his watch chain; the right was deep in the pocket of his coat, and Logan guessed that he held a derringer there.

Kinevan, making his shot at the black eight-ball, glanced up to meet Perris' level stare.

"Game ain't over till the last ball's racked," he said.

"You keep an eye on that eight-ball, mister. Corner pocket."

Kinevan made his shot. The cue-ball caromed off a cushion, tipped the number fifteen ball into a side pocket and, responding to the Texan's deft English, made its curving path across the baize and ivory clicked on celluloid as the eight-ball, timeless symbol of trouble in any man's language, rifled into the designated corner pocket.

"You called your shot neat enough," Perris grinned, speaking around his cigar. "Takes steady nerves, Kinevan. We'll see how you make out with Blackie Marengo, a few minutes from now. He learned the game over at Deer Lodge."

Kinevan missed his next try, racked his count and moved his cue up to the wooden buttons on the overhead wire to adjust his score.

"I'll have to give Blackie a handicap," Logan said, his eyes belying the innocuous words. "Last time I saw him he had a broken arm."

Finishing his run, Logan racked the balls he had dropped. He thought wildly, How long is Perris going to play this cat and mouse game? He must be waiting for Marengo to show up.

Turning away from the wall rack, neither Kinevan nor Perris was aware that Cleve Logan had concealed the celluloid eight-ball in his palm. Approaching Kinevan, Logan saw that his friend was keyed to the breaking point, his knuckles white as he gripped the maple cue.

Logan knew what was in Kinevan's mind. The cowhand's glance flicking toward the nearest of the curtained windows within range of his pool cue telegraphed his intentions. One swipe of the cue could demolish the ceiling lamp over this table, plunge the room into instant blackness. Another swipe of the hardwood butt would smash open a path to get away through that window. And draw Duke Perris' certain fire.

That was the play Kinevan was planning. That was the move Perris no doubt expected. The big speculator was watching them both with a hard intensity, every muscle taut, waiting, waiting.

"I'm out of pipe tobacco, Tex," Cleve Logan said, deliberately putting himself between Kinevan and the window. "How about one of those stogies?"

Anticlimax shot across Kinevan's eyes as he fumbled in his vest for a cigar and handed it over. Something in Logan's eyes as their hat brims touched warned the Texan that Logan was figuring another angle here.

Biting off the end of the cigar, Logan leaned his cue against the pool table and reached up to the suspended lamp with his left hand, pulling it down on its counterbalanced chains.

With the shadow of his hat brim falling on his right hand and the eight-ball palmed there, Logan jacked up the hot globe of the lamp and, leaning forward across the mahogany rim of the table, touched the tip of his cigar to the wick flame.

Tex Kinevan, deducing that this seemingly innocent business was somehow fraught with critical import for

161

them both, forced his eyes off the pulled-down lamp which Logan's left hand held at face level.

Under the pretense of getting his cigar going freely, Logan let the celluloid eight-ball roll out of his cupped palm, into the brass cowling which housed the lamp's wick-spreader. Screening this maneuver behind dense puffs of cigar smoke, Logan lowered the chimney on its prongs and let the counter-balance weights lift the lamp back to its place under the ceiling.

At that elevation, no eye could see the highly inflammable pool ball which Logan had left inside the lamp chimney, an inch from the open flame.

From somewhere in the recesses of his memory, Cleve Logan had dredged up a picture from out of the past—the time a drunken cowhand in a Montana saloon had chucked a similar pool ball into a heating stove. The resulting explosion of the celluloid sphere had shattered the cast iron stove to bits, scattering embers which had burned the building to its foundations.

The intolerable strain was beginning to show on Kinevan, for his next shot missed a pat setup by inches. Waiting for the cue ball to finish its angling journey around the rubber cushions, both men heard the sound of a side door opening and closing, and it seemed to them in that moment that the temperature of this smoke-fouled poolroom dropped by ten degrees.

Logan heard Tex Kinevan suck in a breath at his shoulder as he crouched over the table, studying his next shot. Glancing up under the downsweep of his Stetson brim, Cleve Logan saw the big shape of

Blackie Marengo standing there.

Marengo's right arm was reposing in a sling. His left was filled with a big-bored Remington six-shooter, its knurled hammer tipped back to full cock.

Logan straightened up, restraining an almost irresistible urge to glance up at the lamp. It seemed impossible that the eight-ball nested against the hot metal wick housing had not heated up to the detonation point by now. He knew a moment's panic, wondering if the pool ball was made of some non-inflammable composition, perhaps ivory enameled black.

"All right, men," Duke Perris spoke, lifting a stubby-barreled .41 derringer from his coat pocket. "This farce has continued long enough. I could have tallied you over at Ringbone tonight, Logan. I brought you here to face Marengo first."

Kinevan was standing at Logan's side, every muscle in his rawhide frame bulging with strain as he chalked his cue tip. A rivulet of sweat trickled off the point of his chin as he heard Logan's half-whisper, "Take it easy, kid. Wait this out."

Blackie Marengo was grinning at Logan with pure venom in his eyes. Duke Perris moved over beside the convict, his gaze directed now at Tex Kinevan.

"You told Toke Grossett that Logan was Trig Fetterman," Perris said. "That's why I'm forced to scratch you off, Kinevan."

Cleve Logan spoke desperately, "My error there, Perris. I wasn't sure you'd taken my bait. I got Kinevan to do that to help establish my little masquerade. Kinevan's not mixed up in this."

Perris grinned. "He's not wearing a star?"

Logan shook his head. "Kinevan is an old friend, not a lawman. He had the bad luck to run into me on the *Sacajawea*. I deserve to be stirrup-drug through hell for sucking him in."

Perris turned to his gorilla-faced henchman.

"Blackie, you take Logan. I'll cash in Kin—"

In that instant an earsplitting blast came from the innards of the big ceiling lamp overhead. The eight-ball's delayed explosion was a cataclysmic thing in this confined room, plunging the place into deep and instantaneous blackness, the air filled with flying shards of glass and twisted metal from the blasted lamp.

Logan hurled his cue like a harpoon at the flash of bore-flame which spat from Blackie Marengo's big .44. He felt the concussion wave of the explosion strike his eardrums; the blow of that was a physical thing, as acutely painful as a nail being pounded through his temples; and it seemed that instantaneously the poolroom was choked with celluloid fumes.

Splashing coal oil from the lamp's ruptured tank sprayed Logan as he spun on his heel, reaching in the darkness for Kinevan.

He was pushing Kinevan toward the window when he heard the flat discharge of Duke Perris' derringer, followed by a shocked lurch on Kinevan's part as the .41 ball hit him a solid blow.

So brief had been the elapsed time that the first clatter of falling debris from the wrecked lamp was only now raining on the pool table and floor. In that moment Logan felt Kinevan sag to his knees, his head thumping into the window sill.

The drawn window blind protected Logan's shoulder as he smashed bodily through that opening, sending glass fragments and splintered sash into the alley outside.

Hoisting Kinevan's sagging bulk over his shoulder, Logan half-lunged, half-fell through the window, the windstorm's blast putting its cold touch on him as he and Kinevan hit the ground with jarring impact.

Marengo's .44 was hammering out shots as Logan got to his feet, aware that Kinevan was either dead or unconscious, giving him no help.

With the wind's thrust at his back, Logan staggered down the alley in a zigzag run, bent low under Kinevan's bulk. He remembered the Ringbone riders Buckring had left out here, but as his feet hit the first up-angle of the hill he knew he had somehow escaped those guards if they had been waiting behind the Palace.

Above the roar of the storm Logan thought he heard following shots, but it was blood beating in his ears. He had to lower Kinevan to the ground to get a fresh hold on the Texan, and as he resumed his slogging flight up the hill he heard Kinevan's cry, "Drop me an' vamose, kid. I'm past savin'."

Resting here was too risky. By now Perris and Marengo would either be in pursuit or would have Buckring's men questing the night in search of their escaped quarry.

Kinevan was unconscious now. The back of his shirt was drenched with warm blood, dripping onto Logan's supporting arm.

Holding Kinevan in his arms like a child, Logan slogged blindly up hill, steering for the yellow nimbus of light which marked a house window up there.

He lost all sense of direction. That lighted window might prove to be haven or trap; with a badly wounded, perhaps dying man to think of, he would have to make that gamble.

He passed a fence gate that was slamming and banging in the wind's blast and stumbled to a stone doorstep. He heard Kinevan emit an anguished groan as the wounded man's shoulders hit the door panels.

Logan was shifting Kinevan's heavy burden in his arms, making ready to rap his boot toe on the door, when it opened and Alva Ames stood framed there, holding a hurricane lamp shoulder high.

"Let me come in, Alva," Logan panted. "Tex has been shot."

He felt a mixture of relief and anxiety surge through him as he realized that his blind, stumbling flight away from the Palace Casino had led him to Jebediah Ames' church parsonage.

16: VOICE OF A KILLER

Alva Ames put her full weight against the door to force it shut against the pressure of the dust-laden gale as Logan lurched into the welcome warmth of the room.

"Opal told me you were in danger," the girl was saying, her words barely reaching Logan above the storm's roar outside. "I tried to reach you at the ranch. I failed you, Cleve."

Logan's glance took in the room, one edge of his mind marveling at the transformation it had undergone from a shambles of dirt and disorder to this neat, feminine room with curtains at the windows, hook rugs on the floors.

"This way—my bedroom," Alva said, hurrying past him to open a door on their left. "Jeb, bring a kettle of water. Mr. Logan has brought a wounded man here."

Logan saw the spare figure of the blind parson emerge from the kitchen, then wheel back immediately to do his sister's bidding. Logan carried Kinevan's limp weight into Alva's bedroom and lowered him gently on a blanket as the girl pulled aside a chenille spread.

"This is a doctor's job," Logan panted hoarsely, afraid of what he saw in Kinevan's ashen face. "Do you know if Owlhorn has a . . ."

"Doctor Nease. He lives in the next cabin up the hill," the girl broke in. "I'll bring him."

Jebediah Ames appeared in the bedroom doorway with a steaming copper kettle an instant after his sister hurried through it. Logan heard the back door slam, felt a rush of cold air as Alva raced out into the storm on her errand.

"Reverend, put all the pots of water you have on to boil," Logan ordered the blind man, taking the kettle from him. "That's the first thing a medico will call for."

Tex Kinevan's eyes flickered open as Logan was stemming the flow of blood from the bullet hole over the cowhand's left kidney, using a wad of linen he had ripped from a bedsheet.

"You don't belong here, kid," the Texan's feeble whisper reached Logan. "You come out here to dab your twine on Perris. You better go scoutin' for that rat before he skins out."

Logan got the hemorrhage stopped for the time being. His throat had a swelling ache in it and his words came hard.

"I got you into this thing, Tex. I ought to be shot."

Kinevan closed his eyes and his white lips twitched in a ghost of his old indolent smile.

"Nice play down there in the poolroom. Didn't think we had a chance."

Kinevan's voice trailed off on a diminishing scale and the man's painful shudders relaxed as a merciful coma blanked out his senses. Somewhere in the back part of the house Logan listened to Jebediah Ames priming a pump, getting a supply of water ready to heat.

Having done what he could for the wounded puncher, Logan made the rounds of the windows in bedroom and living room and secured the blinds. He stepped outside the front door and stood keening the storm-whipped darkness for any trace of the man-hunters he knew Perris and Buckring would have searching the night.

Going back inside he heard Jeb Ames greeting his sister and the Owlhorn medical practitioner, who had entered from the kitchen in the rear.

Some vagrant impulse made Logan grope under his levis to unpin the marshal's badge he had worn concealed there, affixing it to his shirt as Alva and the cowtown doctor entered the room. The goat-whiskered old medico was carrying a black kit and he had only the briefest of glances for Logan as he followed Alva into the bedroom and took his first look at the wounded man on the bed.

"If this man dies it will be a murder case, Doc," Logan said, watching as the doctor spread out his scalpels and hemostats on a sterile towel. "Can you give me any hope to go on?"

Dr. Nease's skilled fingers cleaned Kinevan's bullet-torn tissues with a wad of alcohol soaked cotton.

"I'll probe for that slug," Nease said without looking up, "but offhand I don't give this man a chance to survive the night."

Logan's eyes held their pain and grief as he glanced over to where Alva Ames stood at the foot of the bed, her waist encircled by her brother's arm. The sky-pilot's lips were moving in silent prayer and Logan saw that the girl's eyes were fixed on his law badge with a kind of fierce pride burning in them.

"The parson and Alva are in personal jeopardy as long as the patient remains under their roof, Doctor," Logan said anxiously. "Is there anywhere else we could move him for the operation?"

Dr. Nease reached for a probe.

"Impossible as long as this man is in a comatose condition."

Logan's shoulders slumped. "Alva, bolt every door and window in the house. I'm going down to roust the sheriff. We'll deputize a couple of reliable men and post them here to guard the parsonage for the rest of the night."

Turning to leave, Logan saw the doctor glance up at Alva Ames.

"Run over to my place," he ordered the girl, "and tell my wife to fetch a can of chloroform from the office. This man could go into a fatal case of shock if he came to without an anesthetic."

Logan and the girl left the house together, breasting the storm's full fury. Alva headed up the hill toward Nease's place, Logan quartering down the slope toward the blurred lights marking Owlhorn's main street.

Black shapes crossed and recrossed those lights, men moving erratically through the storm's fury; and Logan caught raveling snatches of shouts being exchanged by these men who were hunting the ground behind the Palace.

Those would be Ringbone riders spurred on by Perris and Buckring, most likely. Realizing his danger, with no gun at his hip, Logan broke into a run.

He reached the courthouse square's stake and rider fence and followed it to the brick jail. He found the office lighted but empty. A gun cabinet stood behind the sheriff's desk and Logan broke the lock with a stove poker to open it. Looking over the assortment of rifles and shotguns and side arms which the arsenal contained, Logan selected a coiled shell belt with

170

loops filled with .45 caliber ammunition.

He found a Peacemaker revolver in the collection which Farnick had probably confiscated from former prisoners in his custody, checked the loads and snugged the gun into holster.

He was about to leave the jail office in search of the sheriff when Vick Farnick came in out of the night. Their hands met and clasped, no introduction necessary between these two.

"I let Stagman know you made it here safe, Logan," Sheriff Farnick said. "You mixed up in the ruckus at the Palace tonight?"

Logan recounted the escape from Perris' pool hall trap and the high points in the tangled events which had led up to that episode.

"You've scotched Perris' land grab, at any rate," the sheriff commented when Logan had finished. "That's what Stagman sent you out on this case to do, wasn't it?"

Logan accepted a bottle which Farnick took from his desk, and fortified himself with a quick drink.

"Yes and no," he said. "Stagman wasn't aware of this plot between Perris and Jube Buckring to grab off the river front homesteads for Ringbone. All he knew was that Perris had gone to Lewiston to round up twenty-odd men and was shipping them down the Snake in the *Sacajawea*, bound for Klickitat Landing. My job was to find out what Perris was up to, passing myself off as an escaped convict named Fetterman."

Farnick's rheumy eyes held a bright animation in their mottled depths as he pondered this information.

"How'd Perris get wise to you bein' an impostor?"

Logan told him of Blackie Marengo. Then, realizing that the outlaw was still abroad in the night and that arresting Duke Perris was still a major objective as yet unaccomplished, he said harshly, "We got to work fast, Sheriff. I'll need a couple of deputies to guard the parsonage where Kinevan is. Buckring can wait—he won't drift. I'm not too concerned with those Lewiston flunkies, whether they escape or not. But if Perris makes his getaway I'll be a long time getting rid of this star and going back to my spread in the Blue Mountains."

Farnick blew out the light and they left the jail office, moving up the deserted, wind-hammered street toward the town lodge hall where, Farnick explained, he had men he could deputize to assist in tonight's manhunt.

Reaching the lodge hall, Logan remained in the outer vestibule while the sheriff went in to contact his deputies.

Thus alone with his thoughts for the first time since leaving Kinevan's bedside, Logan recalled what Alva Ames had told him tonight about Opal Waymire's efforts to warn him of the trap Perris was laying for him and Kinevan here in town.

The mystery of Alva Ames' abortive attempt to reach the Ringbone this morning was explained now; she had been trying to carry Opal's message to him. Shifting her allegiance from Duke Perris was a thing that Logan could not fully understand in Opal Waymire; it had involved terrible personal risk and it could only have been engendered by some real feeling that he had roused in the honkytonk girl.

The run of Logan's thoughts was interrupted by the return of Sheriff Farnick and two men whom he introduced as Gulbrandsen and Hartnig.

In the gloom of the lodge hall vestibule, Logan explained to the two deputies that their business would be to maintain an all night guard at the Ames parsonage, to protect Kinevan against any attack by Perris or Buckring's men.

When Gulbrandsen and Hartnig had departed on their mission, the sheriff and Cleve Logan paused indecisively outside the lodge hall.

"Perris could be anywhere in this storm," Logan said. "We'll try his room behind the land office, in case he decides to go through with this deal of filing premature claims on those river strip homesteads and collect Buckring's pay."

The sheriff gripped Logan's arm and leveled a bony hand toward the Federal land office, directly opposite them. The twin windows of the little shack were aglow with light and through the storm's driving dust they could see Gus Gulberg's pudgy figure seated at his desk, engrossed in a dossier of papers.

"How about arrestin' that land agent here an' now, for a starter?" Farnick asked. "If Gulberg's in this as deep as Perris or Buckring, we'd—"

Logan shook his head. "Gulberg's in the clear until we catch him redhanded making out homestead papers in advance of the government's due date."

Logan pulled the sheriff into the black archway of a

livery barn which gave them a view of Gulberg's office.

"I have a hunch Duke Perris won't try a getaway until he's made his deal with Buckring," Logan said. "He can't do that without drawing Gulberg out of his office. I'd say our best bet would be to give up the idea of hunting down Perris and wait for him to send for Gulberg. I'd stake my last blue chip that Gulberg's waiting for just that."

At that moment Duke Perris was standing in the shelter of a storm-tossed juniper midway up the hill overlooking the roof of the Palace Casino.

From that vantage point Perris had a full view of the house where Dr. Lawrence Nease, the town's only doctor, made his home. A moment before, Alva Ames and the doctor's wife had left the house and were heading at a run in the direction of Nease's office on the main street. And this strange nocturnal haste on the part of the two women took on a significant importance to Duke Perris.

Waiting until the two women had disappeared down the hill, Perris approached the doctor's home and came to an unshuttered window. Through that opening he convinced himself that Nease was not at home.

Nothing short of an emergency case could have taken the old medico away from the comfort of his fireside on a night like this.

Perris was certain that he had killed Cleve Logan at the instant of the deputy's escape through the pool hall window; at such short range the derringer couldn't miss. He wondered now if Kinevan had carried Logan somewhere, wounded, and had sent for Owlhorn's doctor to attend the man.

On a hunch, Perris slanted along the hill to the rear of the Ames' parsonage. Testing the doorknob, he found it unlocked. Holding a cocked six-shooter in his right hand, the speculator eased the door open cautiously and stepped inside.

Two doors faced him. One gave Perris a view of a darkened bedroom off to the right. The other led into the living room.

A subdued mutter of voices reached Perris' ear from the front part of the house, followed by approaching footsteps. Perris moved quickly into the unlighted bedroom, just as Dr. Nease came into the kitchen and headed toward the cookstove.

A crack of light immediately ahead revealed a second bedroom, from which the sound of voices had come. Perris skirted the edge of a dimly-seen cot and opened that door a crack, peering into the further bedroom.

A man, stripped to the waist, lay belly-down on the bed there. Jebediah Ames knelt beside the unconscious man, shielding his face from Perris' view; the blind man was holding a retractor in place where the doctor had made an incision in the patient's back. The room reeked with the smell of blood and antiseptic.

Then Perris realized that the man was Kinevan, not Logan; and he concluded that Marengo's shots had wounded the cowpuncher, who must have dropped Cleve Logan's body somewhere down the hill on his way to this place.

The absence of chloroform odors in this room told Perris that the man he had shot down in the Palace was not under an anesthetic. Obviously, the doctor was in the process of probing for Perris' derringer slug.

If Kinevan regained consciousness even for a moment, his word before witnesses could pin a murder charge on Duke Perris. And during his long career of outlawry, Perris had never given the law any tangible proof of his criminal dealings. Next to deputy marshal Cleve Logan, this unconscious man on the bed was Perris' most dangerous enemy.

Out in the kitchen behind him, Perris could hear the doctor stoking the cookstove. Perris had only to worry about Jebediah Ames as a witness of what he intended to do here. And Jebediah Ames was a blind man.

Perris opened the door wider and slid the barrel of his Colt along the wooden door frame. He spoke softly, "Ames, move around."

The blind minister started violently as he heard the voice coming from his own bedroom doorway. Straightening up, he no longer formed a shield between Kinevan and Perris' gun.

"What?" Jebediah Ames exclaimed. "Who is it? Who's there?"

With cold precision, Perris aimed his Colt at Kinevan's head and squeezed the trigger. He saw the cowpuncher's head roll violently on the pillow to the shock of the point blank bullet.

Raw gunsmoke smote the blind skypilot's face in a thick smudge. His super-sensitive ears caught the faint pad of the intruder's feet moving back, the door closing with a slight thud.

The blast of the gunshot brought Dr. Nease racing through the living room from the kitchen. The medical man stood aghast in the doorway of Alva's room, staring through the gunsmoke's stirring layers at the murdered man on the bed. Kinevan was beyond his help now, irrevocably and finally.

A cold draft against his neck nape told the doctor that Kinevan's murderer had left the house by the back door.

After a long moment, the doctor stepped past the frozen shape of Jebediah Ames and pulled a blanket over Kinevan's bleeding head.

"Only the fact that you were blind saved you from being shot down, Reverend," the doctor said huskily. "This man is dead."

Jebediah Ames groped a shaking hand over the blanket to grip Kinevan's fingers.

"God have mercy on your soul," he whispered.

Ames stood up, turning his scarred face toward the doctor.

"I heard the killer's voice speak an instant before that shot was fired, Doctor," the blind man said. "I could identify that voice if I ever heard it again. It belonged to one of the men I heard talking during the voyage of the *Sacajawea* down the Columbia River last week. I'm almost certain it was the voice of Duke Perris."

Spying on Gus Gulberg's office became an intolerable thing to Cleve Logan, crouched in the livery stable's archway with Farnick hunkered at his elbow.

His over-active mind was deviled by conflicting possibilities. What if Perris had decided against going through with his land grab deal and at this moment might be riding across the Horse Heaven Hills, taking advantage of the dust storm to escape Owlhorn forever?

On the other hand, what possible chance was there of hunting Perris or Buckring down in the black fury of the night? It was an impossible stalemate, an enforced interval of inaction which might bring them a showdown or prove wholly futile.

The whipping wind carried the ammoniac reek of the stable against their backs, put a chill to the marrow of their bones as time ran on, growing into an hour. Only the figure of the government land agent, still waiting in his lighted office across the street, kept Cleve Logan chained to his tracks.

Gulberg was waiting for something; it wasn't logical that he should be working through the wee hours this way. Upon Gulberg's duplicity depended the entire outcome of this land grab outrage with its terrible consequences for the unsuspecting homesteaders who were waiting for Monday's opening date to set the land rush in motion.

"Damn John Stagman," muttered the sheriff, starting

to roll a smoke and then realizing he could not light a cigarette and thus betray their vigil here. "Why didn't the marshal handle this job himself, instead of draggin' you into it?"

Logan shifted position to ease the throbbing ache in his bones. His eyes smarted from peering across the dusty street at Gulberg's window for so long a time, not knowing whether this vigil was a waste of precious time or not.

"Perris knew Stagman; he didn't know me. My work as a deputy kept me in Montana where Perris has never operated. We were sure Perris didn't know that Fetterman had been cornered and shot in Pendleton, a month ago. I tallied close enough to Fetterman's description on the reward posters to fool Perris. Besides, I owed Stagman another fling behind the star. He sold me my Blue Mountain ranch for a song last year."

Farnick chewed on his mustache for a moment, fighting his own personal battle with his keyed-up nerves.

"For Stagman's sake, I hope we nab Perris tonight," Logan went on. "He's watched Perris put over crooked oil stock deals in Oklahoma and salted mines in Colorado, but he's never been able to pin anything tangible on him. The man's slippery as a—"

Farnick suddenly rose to his feet. "Hold on!" he cried. "There goes Hartnig an' Gulbrandsen comin' out of Prosser Street. Didn't you tell them to guard the parsonage all night?"

Struck by a sudden prescience of disaster, Logan

and the sheriff bolted out of their hiding place and slanted across Main Street to intercept the two deputies, just as they rounded the corner in front of the Palace Casino.

"Somebody sneaked into the parsonage an' shot Kinevan in cold blood," Hartnig answered their query. "The blind preacher said he'd know the killer's voice if he heard it again—thinks it was Perris. We waited until Miss Ames an' her brother went over to Doc Nease's to spend the night, an' then pulled out. No sense in playin' guard to a dead man, is there, Sheriff?"

Cleve Logan stood rigid in a well of cold shock and anger as his mind ran back across the years, recalling the boyhood he and Tex Kinevan had spent together in Wyoming's Bighorn country. Now that friend of yesteryear was dead, drawn into a business which had been Logan's responsibility alone.

"Son," old Farnick said huskily, laying a hand on Logan's arm, "the only thing I can say is that Kinevan didn't die in vain. He died to help save the bacon of all those homesteaders Perris might have robbed. It's a cinch Perris won't go through with his Ringbone deal now."

Logan was staring off up-street, past the glum deputies. Suddenly he jerked his head up.

"Gulberg's office just went dark, Sheriff. Either he's given up waiting or Perris has sent for him. Come on."

Farnick started after Logan at his hobbling gait, then turned to grab Harnig and Gulbrandsen.

"Boys, Logan an' me are fixin' to round up a den of rattlers tonight. You got your guns loaded for bear. I'd take it as a favor if you'd come along and back our play here."

Cleve Logan broke into a run, leaning his body against the storm's unseen barrier as he slogged up the hardpan street toward the government land office.

As Logan made out the dim outlines of the homestead agency by the glare of a further saloon's lights up the street, he caught sight of Gus Gulberg's mountainous shape leave the land office porch and turn abruptly into the adjoining alley. Waiting for him there was a hulking figure Cleve Logan identified as Blackie Marengo.

Logan halted, waiting until Farnick and the two deputies caught up with him.

"Marengo and Gulberg just headed down that alley, Sheriff. Where does it lead?"

Farnick conjured up a quick mental picture of the lay of the land.

"To the alley that cuts behind the Palace and Perris' place."

"Come on. We'll bag some game after all."

Guns ready, the four lawmen approached the alley where the land agent and Perris' man had vanished. On their left was a wheelwright's shop, the only building between Gulberg's office and Perris' headquarters.

Their cautious passage down this alley brought them to the back end of the wheelwright's in time to see lamplight flash briefly from the lean-to behind Perris' land office, as the door opened and quickly closed again.

But that brief whisk of light was sufficient to reveal the destination of Perris' messenger and the crooked land agent.

"Buckring will be in there with Perris' gang of toughs," Logan whispered for the information of the others. "I hadn't hoped that they'd dare pull this off in Owlhorn. We've got to look sharp for any guards Perris has out."

Lights from the upstairs windows of the Palace, where Opal Waymire's percentage girls had their rooms, enabled Logan to lead the sheriff and his two men along the back wall of the wheelwright's shop.

They halted at its far corner, studying the dim light which leaked through holes in the window shades of Perris' living quarters, when a match bloomed briefly behind a man's cupped fingers, betraying the craggy face of one of Jubal Buckring's ranch hands posted alongside the door out of the storm's fury.

Logan charged across the alley, knowing the guard would be temporarily blinded after lighting his cigarette. Gunmetal made its sudden impact on the rider's skull and he went down, his grunt lost under the howl of the wind through the roundabout eaves. Twice more Logan hammered his gun muzzle on his victim's skull to make a sure job of it, then signalled through the blackness for the sheriff and his deputies to cross the alley.

"Gulbrandsen, you take the window," Logan whispered his orders. "Shoot to kill anybody who tries to come through. Hartnig, go up the alley and scout the front end of the building. The sheriff and I will make it a direct play through the door. We've got to push this thing fast."

The two deputies vanished to take their appointed stations. Farnick was at the deputy marshal's elbow as Logan mounted the square back porch facing Perris' door.

Stooping, Logan took a quick squint through the keyhole. Even the limited angle of view afforded by that aperture told him everything he needed to know.

Perris' derelict crew from Lewiston packed the room. Gus Gulberg, his customarily florid face bleached to the color of ash now, was spreading the contents of a brief case on a table.

Silver-haired Jubal Buckring stood in the background, hugging his carpetbag to his chest. At his either elbow stood Blackie Marengo and Duke Perris.

With the sheriff waiting tensely at his side, Logan stooped lower and put an ear to the keyhole. He heard Duke Perris talking rapidly to the men assembled around the table.

"You've got your steamer tickets back to Lewiston. You'll get your final pay-off when you reach Idaho. As soon as you get these papers signed, your job is finished. This storm will furnish cover for you to get through Satus Pass to the river. You'll find Caleb Rossiter waiting with his sternwheeler at Klickitat Landing. Now hurry this along."

Logan heard a nervous shifting of feet inside, a rattle of papers. Gus Gulberg's sleazy voice, high-pitched with the anxiety that had unnerved him, squeaked above the hubbub.

"God's sake, hurry. I don't like this business any more than you do."

Logan stood up, giving his gun cylinder a twirl with his thumb. He grunted his signal to Farnick and then, backing off, put his weight against the door. It was locked.

Logan thrust his Colt against the keyhole and fired. The gun made its flashing report and simultaneously with the bullet reducing the cast iron mortise lock to shards, Logan kicked the door open and leaped into Perris' room behind a jutting gun.

Through fogging gunsmoke which eddied violently in the tug of air currents, Logan and the sheriff shouldered inside, Farnick's twin six guns covering the paralyzed figures of Gus Gulberg and Jubal Buckring.

The closely-massed ranks of Perris' henchmen were frozen there in stunned tableau as they whirled to face the door. In the further shadows Logan saw Blackie Marengo, and he swung his gun on the man.

"This place is surrounded," Logan's voice broke through the wall of silence which followed the blast of his gun. "I want every man to get his arms up and belly against the wall. This play is for keeps."

For a moment terror held the crowd enchained. Then Jubal Buckring let slip his carpetbag and clawed a gun from his coat.

The sheriff let gunhammer drop and his slug caught the Ringbone cattle king in the right eye before he could lift his Bisley .38 for a shot.

In falling, Buckring's body hit the table lamp and extinguished it instantly, plunging the room into blackness.

Men shouted their panic as bedlam seized the room. Gulberg screamed "Don't shoot!" and somewhere behind that moving mass of humanity Farnick and Cleve Logan heard a door being kicked open to give access to Perris' front office.

Both lawmen held their fire, knowing that to shoot into the packed dark would be wanton slaughter. They braced themselves to meet the onslaught of jostling bodies, ready to lash out with clubbing gun barrels as they heard the table upset and furniture being smashed to matchwood by struggling bodies.

Out front the street door opened, letting the storm's blast have its full and uninterrupted sweep through the building. A spate of gunfire beat up rolling echoes in that direction and Logan knew Hartnig was shooting it out with escaping men.

Then the firing ceased and the room was silent save for the furtive scrape of boots and the chorus of men's labored breathing, like saw cuts behind the darkness.

Farnick and Logan separated, putting the wall to their backs. From the gloom Logan's voice lashed out, "Somebody strike a match. Make it fast."

The quavering voice of old Pegleg Cochran chattered out, "Hold your fire, son. I'll give you a light."

Cochran's match spurted from the far left corner. The rising glow revealed a ludicrous picture of men sprawled on the floor like sheep. Gus Gulberg was a trembling mound of fat entangled in the broken legs of the table, half concealed under the spilled legal papers from his brief case.

The big shape of Jubal Buckring lay in a grotesque sprawl beside Gulberg. Blood trickled from the bullet hole under his eyebrow.

"Cochran," Logan addressed that oldster, "light the lamp on that shelf yonder."

As the one-legged derelict complied, Cleve Logan swept the pandemonium-struck room a second time, ignoring the trembling Lewiston riffraff. This search confirmed his first impression. Two men had made their escape from the trap, by way of the outer office. Duke Perris and Blackie Marengo. Unless the deputy had tallied them in the act of escaping to the street.

Leaving Farnick to hold these men under the threat of his guns, Logan passed through the length of the building to reach the open door. Glancing outside, he saw Hartnig's still shape, gun in hand, stretched out on the porch.

Visibility was too restricted here on the street to give any clue as to which way Perris and Marengo had fled after shooting down Hartnig.

Oppressed by a sense of failure, Logan returned to the back room where Gulbrandsen had joined the sheriff.

"Take these swine down to the jail, Sheriff," the deputy marshal said glumly. "Leave Buckring here for the coroner to pick up. They got Hartnig."

Staring down at the dead Ringbone rancher, something else impinged itself on Logan's eye. Buckring's carpetbag was missing. Perris, then, had had the guts to snatch up the bag containing the rancher's pay-off before joining Marengo in a getaway.

18: AMBUSH AT DAWN

Mitzi LaMotte of the Palace Casino was a faded enchantress of indeterminate age. Salvaging her vanished beauty for the customers took considerable artful use of powder puff and rouge jar to conceal the ravages of time and the youth-eroding demands of her profession.

From four o'clock until the Palace closed its doors, usually around sunrise, Mitzi LaMotte and her scarlet sisters cruised the floor of the Palace dance hall, enticing the trade barward where she matched their drinks with sips of tea that looked like whiskey.

If a patron was well-heeled financially or was sufficiently in his cups, Mitzi LaMotte was expected, for a certain percentage of the proceeds, to either signal the bartender to include chloral hydrate crystals in his next drink—in which case the patron wound up in the back alley with a sore skull and a missing purse—or, in the case of Owlhorn regulars from the Ringbone or other ranches, who might resent a repetition of such drastic treatment, Mitzi would use her feminine wiles to persuade her victim to visit the Palace's roulette layout, rondo-coolo games or chuckaluck cages.

Tonight business had gone sour. An explosion of unknown origin in the back poolroom had frightened out most of the sodbusters in the house. Much later, an outbreak of gunfire next door had finished emptying the Palace.

This was shortly after three o'clock in the morning. Opal Waymire, the new proprietress of the deadfall, had her floormen empty the barroom of such drunks as were incapable of locomotion and make the rounds blowing out lamps. This was the signal which permitted the Palace dance hall girls to retire to their sleeping rooms on the upper floor, to spend the following daylight hours in the oblivion of well-earned slumber.

Mitzi LaMotte, fitting her key into the lock of Room 12 at the extreme end of the upstairs hall, was not too far gone with weariness to notice that some unknown intruder had, sometime this evening, kicked the door in. Too physically depleted to bother her head about what belongings she might find stolen, Mitzi limped into the room and kicked off her gold pumps with their tinsel pompoms.

Hobbling painfully on feet which had taken their usual bruising from cowpunchers' Justins and homesteaders' clodhopper brogans, Mitzi crossed over to her dresser, fished in a tray of hairpins for a match, and lighted the brass lamp in its wall sconce beside the blemished mirror.

She was in the act of removing a switch from her hair when her blousy eyes focused on the image of a man reflected in the mirror, a man standing with his back to the door she had just closed. The man was Duke Perris' henchman, Blackie Marengo.

Mitzi LaMotte wheeled around to face the roughneck, her painted lips twisting as she ground out a bar-room obscenity.

"You've come to the wrong room, Blackie. There's no red light burning over my door. Get out!"

Blackie Marengo leered as he gave the girl's lumpy figure a discriminatory appraisal.

"You flatter yourself, you washed-out slut. Go downstairs and send Opal Waymire up here. And don't let any of the girls know I sent you or I'll wring your skinny neck."

Mitzi reached behind her to pick up a heavy silver hairbrush. This man did not appear to be drunk and, having recently assumed Toke Grossett's role as Duke Perris' bodyguard, was due a respect not enjoyed by the average Palace customer.

"You go to hell, Blackie," Mitzi retorted, brandishing the hairbrush like a club. "I'm tired out. You want Opal, go fetch her your own self."

Blackie Marengo reached for the rubber-stocked .44 slung for cross-draw at his flank. The hammer made its ominous double click as he thumbed it back to full cock.

"Rattle your hocks before I shoot your ears off."

Mitzi LaMotte fled for the doorway and her bare feet pattered off down the corridor.

At this juncture the curtains which partitioned off a corner wardrobe closet stirred and Duke Perris emerged into the glare of lamplight. Slung across one arm was the carpetbag which the late Jubal Buckring had brought out from the Ringbone.

Hearing a commotion out on the street, the fugitive

promoter crossed the shabby cubicle and tipped back a corner of a green window shade for a look at the street below.

"Well, there goes the sheriff with Gulberg and our Lewiston friends," commented Perris indifferently. "By the time they get through squealing Logan will have enough evidence to put a bounty on my top-knot."

Blackie Marengo, guarding the door of Room 12, shifted the weight of his splinted arm in the greasy sling, worry furrowing the corners of his deep-socketed eyes.

"Every minute we stay here, the more our chances of stretchin' hemp, boss," the convict grumbled. "What's to hold us? Five gets you fifty Logan's already got this saloon surrounded with vigilantes."

Perris turned from the window, his tall frame wholly at ease except for the hand which plucked nervously at his gold bullet luck piece. His ruddy face was paler than usual, making the tobacco-colored freckles stand out like polka dots.

"What chance would we have had to fork a horse?" he demanded testily. "Ten to one the sheriff had every livery barn in town guarded. Besides, I'm not pulling out and leaving Opal behind."

A sound of high-heeled slippers coming up the outer hall brought Marengo wheeling around to face the door, gun in hand. The door swung open and Opal Waymire, dressed in a revealing satin gown of emerald green garnished with sparkling brilliants, stepped into Room 12. Her heavily mascaraed eyes were round and full of fear as Duke Perris walked across the room and kissed her.

The girl's iron self-control wavered for a moment and she leaned against the big man's shoulders, her body quivering.

"It's all right, Opal," Perris consoled her. "I thought we'd killed or wounded Logan and we hadn't. But Blackie and I got away with Buckring's pay-off, so we got what we came to Owlhorn for."

Opal Waymire plucked a wispy lace handkerchief from the cleft of her bosom and dabbed at her eyes as Perris stepped back and lifted Buckring's carpetbag before her.

"Better than a hundred thousand in greenbacks in this bag, Opal. Easy to carry. What difference if we leave Gulberg and those Lewiston bums to fry in their own juice? Logan's got nothing he can hang me for."

Opal Waymire lurched over to Mitzi LaMotte's bed and slumped down on it. She turned her tragic eyes on Perris and whispered huskily, "That's where you're wrong, Duke. You overstepped yourself tonight, leaving a dead man behind you."

Perris laughed softly. "I didn't shoot Buckring, if that's what the talk is. Farnick did that. He wouldn't frame that killing on me."

Opal shook her head. "No, Duke. I heard the talk outside. You killed Tex Kinevan. Logan will hunt you to the ends of the earth to avenge his friend."

A break came in Duke Perris' insouciant calm. His eyes shot over to Blackie Marengo and back to the girl. "Who says I killed Kinevan?"

"Logan himself."

"That's a damned lie. I mean, he's bluffing, Opal. I shot Kinevan. I had to get rid of him. But my only witness was Jeb Ames and he's blind."

Opal said, "But he isn't deaf, Duke. Jeb Ames says he heard the voice of Kinevan's murderer and he's almost positive it was your voice. If he ever heard you speak again, Duke, the jig would be up. There isn't a judge or jury in the land that wouldn't take the sworn testimony of a clergyman, especially a blind clergyman."

Perris dragged a sleeve across cheeks that suddenly glistened with sweat.

"All right," he said, desperation touching his voice. "The reason I sent for you was to get help, Opal. We've got to get out of Owlhorn tonight. Before this storm lets up. Is the Palace under guard yet?"

"By now it is. Logan and the sheriff are going to search this building as soon as they get their prisoners in jail. You haven't more than five minutes, Duke."

Perris took a quick turn around the floor.

"We'll go through the wine cellar and out the ventilator shaft, Marengo," he told his bodyguard. "Opal, have one of the bouncers get horses for us and picket them in the ravine back of the church."

Opal heaved herself off the bed. At the door she turned to put her imploring eyes on Perris.

"You—you are taking me with you, aren't you, Duke?"

He kissed her, with a tenderness that was rare in him. "Later. It would be best if you were around while the law is searching the Palace. Come on. We can't be trapped upstairs."

They left Mitzi LaMotte's room, going down the unlighted hall and descending the main staircase into the black pit that was the barroom. A rifle-toting guard's shadow was on the colored glass windows in the main street door, proof that Logan had the Palace under guard.

Behind the bar was a trap door which opened on a short flight of steps descending to the wine cellar. Into this redolent gloom Opal and the two men groped, shivering in the dank cold of the subterranean room.

"This is the plan," Perris whispered, holding the girl close. "We've got to figure that Farnick is already burning up the telegraph lines out of Owlhorn, tipping off Yakima and Pasco and every other settlement in a hundred mile radius of here. We can't risk a run through Satus Pass to meet the *Sacajawea* down at the river landing. Our best bet is to head for the hills and lie low a few days till Logan's manhunt cools off."

He felt Opal's breast crushed against him, her shoulders tremoring. "But where then? Where?" she asked frantically.

"Blackie tells me of a place he camped after he left Winegarten's ranch on the river. The ruins of old Fort Rimrock on the bluff overlooking the Columbia. It's a day's ride from here, southeast across the Horse Heaven divide. You'll find it on the county map in your office, Opal. Fort Rimrock. That's where Blackie and I will wait for you to show up in a day or so with food and ammunition. Just make sure you aren't trailed out of Owlhorn."

Opal left them in the wine cellar then, going back up to the barroom to look up a floor man she could trust with the all-important business of getting saddle horses ready for the fugitives.

She was back in a few minutes, invisible in the complete darkness of the cellar.

"Leedom will have the horses waiting beyond the church," she whispered. "With a pair of deer rifles in the boots. When do I join you, Duke?"

"Not tomorrow. You'll be watched. Stick around in plain sight of the town. Logan will question you. Tell him you haven't seen me since the shoot-out tonight. I'll be waiting for you at the fort, Opal. And depending on you."

She clung to Perris for a long moment, kissing him passionately. When they broke apart, conscious of Blackie Marengo's impatient breathing in the darkness, Opal said, "You'd better go now. Logan will be certain to investigate this cellar."

Hooking his arm through the handles of Buckring's carpetbag, Perris groped off into the cellar, feeling his way past tiers of beer kegs and cased liquor in storage here.

A delivery tunnel slanted upward from the cellar, its ground level entrance protected by a plank door locked on the inside. But attempting a getaway by that route would be too risky; if Logan had the Palace exits guarded, he would be sure not to overlook the tunnel door.

A ventilating shaft, the roof of which was overgrown with back lot weeds, was now directly over-head. After a moment's bickering Marengo lifted Perris to his shoulders, heard the speculator opening the louvred vent.

Crawling out into the weeds, Perris leaned down through the ventilator housing to give Marengo a lift out of the tunnel. In a moment they were in the open, searching the night for hostile sounds.

The storm was abating as dawn approached but there was still enough dust flying to obscure their flight as Perris and Marengo scuttled off up the hill-side.

Dawn's first light was a lantern glow in the east as they passed the steepled church and continued on over the hump of the hill into the brushy ravine beyond.

Waiting for them there in a thicket of dwarf locusts were two saddled and bridled horses on picket, a shad-bellied bay gelding and a coal black mustang. Leedom, the Palace bouncer who had taken the horses out of a town stable, was nowhere around. As Opal had promised, the saddle scabbards were filled with .54 calibered Ballard rifles.

Mounting the bay, Perris heard Marengo's suspicious voice, "That bouncer trustworthy, boss? He could sell us out to the law."

Perris said, "Holger Leedom is as square as a section-corner or Opal wouldn't have chosen him. Besides, I've got too much on Leedom for him to dare a double-cross."

They spurred out of the locust clump, day's light beginning to show the roundabout rolling horizon.

The old army outpost Marengo had recommended as a hideout lay to the southeast, some fifty miles distant by crowflight.

"Marengo, wait here!" Duke Perris said suddenly. "I've got one more chore to attend to before I leave Owlhorn behind."

Marengo bit out a profane protest. "If you think you can tally Logan and not draw a posse down on us—"

But Perris was already gone, putting his shad-bellied bay up the ravine slope within view of the church. The spectral glow of the dust-obscured sunrise showed him the dim shape of the parsonage at the opposite corner of the churchyard, and toward that house Perris headed his mount.

Reining up outside the fence when he came abreast of the parsonage, Perris dismounted and pulled the Ballard .54 out of its boot. In the act of climbing the fence he saw a tall, angular figure emerge from the rear door of the parsonage and walk directly toward him, one hand sliding along a rope which was held between stakes as a blind man's guide across the yard. The rope ended at a woodpile.

The man was Jebediah Ames, and he was on his way to get an armful of firewood for cooking breakfast.

Perris drew back, steadying the rifle barrel across the top rail of the fence. He slid a finger through the brass trigger guard, waiting until Jeb Ames had loaded his arms with wood and, keeping one hip on the rope guide fence, turned to retrace his steps to the parsonage.

For a full five seconds, Duke Perris held the blind

clergyman's back under his gunsights. When he squeezed off his shot he did not wait for the wind to sweep the powder smoke aside, but turned to snatch his horse's reins and vault into saddle.

He reached the uphill corner of the churchyard and was behind the shelter of a box elder clump before he saw Dr. Nease and two women—the doctor's wife and Alva Ames—leave the Nease house farther along the ridge to investigate the shot.

Roiling dust clouds blotted out a picture of that group running into the churchyard toward the motionless shape of Jebediah Ames, sprawled over his armload of firewood.

Behind that dust Duke Perris dipped down the far ravine slope to where Blackie Marengo was waiting.

"I cashed in the chips of the only man living who could pin a murder charge on me, Blackie," Perris said. "That'll be a comfort in case I ever find myself behind bars in future."

No one was abroad in this ruddy dawn to see the two riders vanish down the ravine trail, putting Owlhorn behind them forever.

19: INTO THE HILLS

Noon of the new day found Owlhorn Valley basking under an enamel blue sky, scoured clean by the seasonal windstorm.

The opening of the government's former Indian land for settlement was less than twenty-four hours away and already queues of land hunters, many of them who had camped along the Rawhide for nearly a month now, had begun to form along the street in front of Gulberg's land office.

These homestead candidates would take turns throughout this Sunday night ahead holding their places in these lines, each family keeping a representative there.

What the sodbusters did not know was that the Federal registrar, Gus Gulberg, would open his books tomorrow morning as an official already under arrest pending trial for attempting to defraud the government.

The witnesses who would clinch Gulberg's conviction in circuit court were under heavy guard at Sheriff Vick Farnick's jailhouse, riffraff imported from distant Idaho to play their abortive rôles in a land steal plot which had been nipped in the bud only last night.

For Cleve Logan, the morning had been spent in an exhaustive house-to-house search of Owlhorn, a manhunt which had started with the Palace Casino and had extended to the uttermost wagon camp along the river, covering every conceivable hiding place the valley afforded.

The hunt had yielded no trace of the missing Duke Perris or Blackie Marengo, as Logan had expected would be the case. But one thing he knew, at least— the fugitive pair had left town. Now he could only sit back and await the developments of the Territory wide dragnet he had established by telegraph, alerting the law to cover every town and road and trail around the compass from Owlhorn. This chore had kept the local

Overland telegraph operator on duty well past dawn. Knowing Perris, Logan was skeptical of baiting the elusive promoter into any trap.

At noon, physically spent, Logan returned from his check of the riverbank camps and retired to his room at the Pioneer House. He flung himself on his bed fully clothed, and was asleep almost instantly.

It was four o'clock when Logan was shaken awake by grizzled Sheriff Farnick. With the old lawman was Alva Ames, her eyes red-rimmed and swollen from weeping.

"We got another tragedy to report, son," Farnick said gently, as Logan swung his feet off the blankets. "Happened at daybreak this mornin', but you were out scoutin' the river camps so I decided to let you get some shut-eye first."

Logan, half drugged by sleep, came fully awake now, almost knowing from Alva's appearance what the nature of Farnick's evil tidings would be.

"Parson Ames was bushwhacked, Cleve," the sheriff said. "Miss Ames here was fixin' breakfast for Doc Nease, and her brother went over to his woodpile for some kindlin'. He was hit where his suspenders cross from somebody firin' from the fence."

For a moment, Logan was too shocked for coherent reaction. He stood up and put both arms around Alva, pulling her to him, feeling her body constrict with the soundless spasms of her grief.

"The parson didn't know what hit him," Farnick went on. "I scouted the grounds soon as Doc Nease sent the word down about the dry-gulchin'. Found a rimfire .54 ca'tridge in the weeds by the fence, but the wind had wiped out any sign on that hardpan."

His cheek pressed against Alva's brunette head, Logan stared across the room at the sheriff, who stood gaunt-cheeked from his own sleepless night.

"Reckon I know the bore of every long gun in Owlhorn," Farnick went on, ill at ease here. "Nobody I know of owns a .54."

Logan said, "Obviously it was Perris' work, or Marengo's. Duke must have known Jeb Ames could have pinned Kinevan's murder on him if he identified his voice. Perris always covers his tracks thoroughly. Ask John Stagman about that."

Alva disengaged herself from Logan's arms and spoke dully, as if to herself, "Jeb was to have preached his first sermon in Owlhorn this morning. At least Jeb isn't—isn't walking in the dark now."

Logan forgot the presence of the old sheriff beside them, forgot everything except the shining, transcendant faith he saw glowing in the girl's eyes.

Whatever more Alva would have said was cut short by the appearance in the doorway of an over-painted girl who had the look of a dance hall jezebel about her.

"They told me you were up here, Mister Sheriff," the girl said in a brassy monotone. "I—I got something to tell you, and to hell with what happens to me for the telling."

Logan tore his gaze off the stars in Alva's eyes and rasped out to the woman in the doorway, "Who are you? What do you want?"

The girl swung her glance from the sheriff and put

her gaze on the silver star pinned to Logan's shirt.

"My name's Mitzi LaMotte, not that it matters a tinker's dam. What I want the law to know about is that Duke Perris an' Blackie Marengo hid in my room over the Palace right after that shootin' scrape last night."

Logan gave Mitzi LaMotte his sharpest attention.

"We searched every room in that honkytonk, including yours."

Mitzi shrugged her bony shoulders. "Not until after Perris and that ape of a Marengo had left, you didn't. When I finished work at three o'clock Marengo was waiting in my room. He sent me downstairs to get Opal Waymire. Opal told me to wait in her office till she got back. When I finally got to bed it was getting onto daylight. Perris and his plug-ugly were gone. One of the girls across the hall saw them leave. I didn't know until Sonora Belle told me that Perris was in there with Marengo. Perris must have hid in my closet."

Logan reached for his gunbelt looped over a bed post and buckled it on with a weary gesture.

"I believe your story, Mitzi. I'll go over and have a talk with Opal. She must have had a hand in their get-away."

He turned to Alva Ames. "There's not much I can say just now, Alva," he spoke in the softest of tones. "I'll see you later this afternoon. We'll both be burying the best friends we ever had, you and I."

Mitzi LaMotte clutched Logan's sleeve as he brushed past her into the hall.

"Opal would kill me if she knew I squealed," whimpered the percentage girl. "She would break me limb from limb."

Logan smiled. "Where Opal is headed for, she'll be an old gray-haired woman before she's free to molest you, Mitzi. Don't let that worry you."

Leaving the hotel, Logan crossed Main Street to the Palace. A deputy was guarding the padlocked batwings, which Logan unlocked. Wading through the litter of the past night's revelry, Logan reached the door of Opal Waymire's living quarters behind the bar.

That door was unlatched and he stepped into the darkened back room to find Opal asleep on a satin-quilted bed with gilt posts. He awakened her by the expedient of running up the window blinds to let the afternoon's westering sunlight flood the room.

Opal Waymire gasped and sat up, jerking the covers over her filmy nightgown. Her face was devoid of makeup and in this harsh light Logan was disillusioned by the stark depravity he saw limned on the woman's features as she stared at him through eyes alight with fear and dread.

"Opal," Logan said, "you tried to tip me off that Perris was going to trap me in your poolroom last night. Why did you do that, knowing I was on a man-hunt, knowing who I was after?"

The girl's hard eyes searched Logan's unshaven face, calculating her method of parrying this unexpected visit. She swung the bedcovers back and gave Logan a tantalizing glimpse of her seductively-draped body as she reached for the same robe he remembered she had worn on the *Sacajawea* the first time he saw her. The intervening week of elapsed time seemed like an aeon.

"A woman in love," she said, "does unaccountable things."

Logan took out his pipe and loaded it thoughtfully, fully aware of her treacherous charms.

"If you love Duke Perris, why did you betray him?"

Opal dropped her eyes with a spurious shyness. "I didn't say that, Cleve. From the moment I laid eyes on you, throwing your lasso at that river boat—when you kissed me—"

"Cut out the theatrics, Opal." Logan's voice carried a whiplash. "Last night you helped Duke Perris and Blackie Marengo escape town. You laid yourself open to criminal prosecution by that, don't you understand?"

Opal dropped her coquettish pose, reading his inflexible mood. Her eyes held a brittle, reptilian brightness as she glared up at him from her seat on the bed.

"You'd take the word of a little tramp like Mitzi LaMotte?"

Logan lit a match and got his pipe going.

"The word of Mitzi LaMotte can send you to the penitentiary for aiding and abetting a known murderer to escape, Opal."

The girl started to speak but Logan waved her into silence.

"Yes," he went on ruthlessly, "Duke Perris over-

203

stepped himself on this Owlhorn land grab, Opal. In the past, he covered his tracks, let hired guns do his dirty work. John Stagman has spent fifteen years trying to out-fox Perris. But this time we have a murder—two murders to pin on him."

Opal licked her pale lips. "You can't prove anything like that against Duke. You're bluffing, Cleve."

Logan shook his head, putting his sidewise stare on her.

"Perris shot Tex Kinevan—once in the poolroom, a wound which would probably have proved fatal, and again up at the parsonage. And on his way out of town, thanks to your help, Opal, Duke Perris took time out to ambush Jebediah Ames. It takes a pretty low breed of snake to shoot a blind man in the back."

From the look of pure shock on Opal Waymire's face, Logan was positive this was her first knowledge of Ames' murder.

"You no doubt plan to join Perris sooner or later," Logan said. "Mitzi's testimony could delay your departure for some time, unless you want to turn State's evidence. The thing for you to do is to decide in a hurry whether a blind man's killer is worthy of your loyalty, Opal."

Logan saw the girl trembling violently, then draw herself together with an effort. Her eyes avoided his as he walked slowly to the door, hoping against hope that she would tell him now what he wanted to know about Perris' whereabouts.

"I love you, Cleve Logan," she said humbly. "Whatever I did, I did for you. My attempt to warn you about last night's trap should prove that. If—if I hadn't helped Duke get away, he would have killed you."

Logan paused at the doorway, a genuine sympathy easing the hard surface glitter of his eyes.

He said, "You surely realize there is nothing in the cards for you and me, Opal."

The hope that had never been absent from Opal's expressive eyes faded and expired before the man's gaze. In a voice that barely reached his ears across the room, Opal said, "It's Alva, isn't it? She adores you, Cleve, which is one thing a woman can tell about another, even though Alva and I are at opposite ends of the earth. I—I was like her, once."

Logan said briefly, "I'm not putting you under arrest now, Opal, because I figure I owe you that much. But when John Stagman gets here this evening and I turn this case over to him, he'll be around to interview you. I advise you to come clean with Stagman. He has the power to lock you up for a big hunk of a lifetime."

He left her with that, returning to the street. Sheriff Farnick and Alva Ames were waiting in front of the Palace.

"She admitted having helped with their getaway," Logan reported, "but she's not yet ready to confess where Perris will be waiting for her. But if we give Opal enough rope, I think she will lead us to Perris eventually. That's the main reason why I didn't lock her up with the others."

Logan glanced at his watch.

"Stagman's due on the six o'clock stage from Pasco," he said. "I shudder to think of what that salty old cuss will say when he finds out Perris slipped through my fingers."

He offered to escort Alva back to her home, but the grief-stunned girl declined and made her aimless way up the street.

She avoided the town's cemetery at the western limits of Owlhorn, where the coroner had a crew working at the opening of three graves. Jubal Buckring, who had found gunsmoke at the end of his rainbow last night, would occupy one of those graves. She was glad to see that the workmen were putting the graves of Tex Kinevan and her brother side by side in a far section of the cemetery.

The sun was westering toward the remote Cascade peaks when Alva returned to the town after a walk which had taken her across the river bridge and far out across the further prairie.

Emotional strain and the rigor of this exercise had made the girl drowsy and she was thinking of returning to Mrs. Nease's to sleep, knowing she could never set foot inside the parsonage which held so much of tragic memory for her.

She was climbing the hill toward the doctor's home when she saw Opal Waymire emerge from the rear of the Cattleman's Mercantile, accompanied by the storekeeper.

A saddled horse, Buckring's own blue roan, was hitched behind that building out of sight of the street. Alva saw the honkytonk girl mount, noted that Opal Waymire was wearing a riding habit.

She waited in saddle while the storekeeper lashed

two heavy gunnysacks behind her cantle, and then spurred off in the direction of the stage road which snaked into the notch of Satus Pass.

Something like panic seized Alva then. She broke into a run, heading for the stable behind the parsonage. The pinto pony her brother had purchased two days ago was waiting there, beside the empty stall which had housed her own horse, shot out from under her by Ringbone's alert guard on her futile attempt to breach Jubal Buckring's Hole-in-the-Wall.

Saddling up, Alva headed for the Owlhorn jail. She was about to dismount there when she saw Cleve Logan leading his dun out from behind the Pioneer House. Sheriff Vick Farnick was walking beside the deputy marshal, and she saw him hand Logan a pair of glittering handcuffs.

The girl put her horse across the intervening distance and called out frantically, "Cleve, you said if we gave Opal enough rope she'd lead us to wherever Duke Perris is hiding."

Logan grinned back at her.

"I've had Opal watched all afternoon," he said. "She just stocked up on canned grub and ammunition at the Mercantile. I've got the sales slip in my pocket now."

Farnick chuckled at the astonishment in Alva's eyes.

"Opal just left town by the Pass road," the sheriff said. "I'll bet that's what's got you all flustered up, ain't it? Well, you got nothing to worry about. Logan will trail her."

Alva nodded frantically. "She can't have more than a mile head start. I'm certain she's on her way to

Klickitat Landing."

Cleve Logan stepped into saddle and adjusted the walnut stock of the sheriff's .45-70 Winchester which projected from under his right knee.

"Heading Opal off would be easy," the deputy said, "but it's Perris and Marengo we're after, remember. Opal doesn't know I'll be on her trail, but she's cagey. Rather than face Stagman this evening, she decided to leave before dark. But you can bet your bottom dollar she's laying a false trail when she heads into Satus Pass. Perris and Marengo didn't head that way."

Logan backed his horse away, looking down at the sheriff.

"Give my regards to Stagman when the stage rolls in," he said, "and keep an eye on Alva here. I may be gone a few days, but I'll be back with big game."

Logan roweled the dun into a gallop from a standing start, leaving Alva Ames and the sheriff in the dust of his pony's hoofs.

Something in the taut fixture of Alva's following gaze caused the sheriff to make a belated and futile reach for the bit of the pinto's bridle.

As if she had anticipated Farnick's intervention, Alva spurred her horse sharply away and called back, "I'm going with Cleve, Sheriff. And don't try to stop me."

The girl slapped her pony's withers with the end of her reins and through the stirred dust old Vick Farnick saw her lining out down the street of false fronts past the lineups in front of Gulberg's land office, following Cleve Logan toward the Pass road and the sunset's golden glory.

Midnight found Opal Waymire at the summit of Satus Pass, the lights of the Wells-Fargo relay station glowing in the darkness at the foot of the south grade.

Traffic was light on this back road through the Horse Heavens as a rule, but three times tonight she had been forced to put her horse off the road to avoid being seen. Once by the Owlhorn stage inbound from Klickitat Landing; again by a platoon of blue-coated cavalry troopers heading to town from Fort Simcoe; and lastly by a string of jerkline mules drawing a tandem-hitched freight wagon train loaded with a consignment of whiskey for her own saloon.

Only the dread of meeting John Stagman had driven Opal Waymire into such a rash thing as leaving Owlhorn in full daylight. She had fully expected to be trailed out of the cowtown, which was why she had made this false tangent away from the direction of her true destination; but so far as she knew, Owlhorn had ignored her departure, perhaps assuming she was taking one of her habitual rides at dusk before starting the night's work at the Palace.

Cleve Logan was in her thoughts as she traveled up the Pass tonight. The knowledge that she would never see him again put a poignant sense of loss in her.

Remembering Alva, Opal Waymire experienced something close to jealousy, but she put aside what might have been, storing her memories of Cleve

Logan along with the other shattered dreams of a tarnished past.

Now, having gained the crown of the Horse Heaven range, the girl was physically exhausted from these unaccustomed miles in the saddle. Here at the summit, the bedrock had been stripped of its volcanic topsoil by the erosion of the ages, and Opal knew that she must leave the main road at this point if she was to throw off any possible trackers who might be on her trail tonight or tomorrow.

This was literally a crossroads in Opal Waymire's checkered and disillusioned worldly existence. To follow these wheel tracks to the Columbia River settlements might bring escape from Washington Territory and the oblivion of Oregon or California, a chance to pick up the disordered remnants of her life in some new scene, under some assumed name.

But she remembered Duke Perris and that man's malignant grip on her heartstrings, the joys as well as the disappointments of the years she had followed his evil star, sharing the uncertainties of his uneasy existence living by his wits, feeling the pressure of a woman living just outside the law's reach.

Studying her choice with a cold detachment, Opal Waymire knew that her destiny was inextricably interwoven with Perris', that it was in the cards that she must rein off the Owlhorn road at this spot and cut eastward along the rolling divide toward the abandoned cavalry post where her man and Blackie Marengo would be waiting, depending for their own escape on the supplies she was bringing.

She waited for long minutes here on the breeze-swept summit, probing the starlit night for any sound of pursuit from the north and hearing none. Here under the Milky Way, Opal Waymire felt the lonesomeness of her misbegotten life pressing in about her, as if she were stranded for eternity in some sterile crater of the moon.

Being a woman with a woman's weaknesses as well as strength, Opal had her temporary release in tears. When the emotional upsurge had spent itself, she picked up her reins and sent the blue roan picking its way up the roadside rocks, secure in the knowledge that the last visible tracks she had left were behind her in the stage road's dust.

Dawn of the day which ushered in the month of June and brought the opening of Owlhorn Valley's coveted public lands found Opal Waymire alone in a dead world of sage and bunchgrass.

To the south lay the shadowy chasm of the Columbia's gorge, twisting its way to a tryst with the sea. Beyond that shadow lay Oregon; at her back were the snowy sawteeth of the Cascades above their mantle of timber, with Mount Adams' ice-crusted pile duplicated by St. Helen's perfect cone further to the west.

She made a dry camp in a sheltered coulee, emptied a canteen in her hat crown to assuage the roan's thirst, and put the horse on picket. In her haste to leave Owlhorn behind her she had forgotten to bring along blankets, and the best bed she could fashion for herself was a mattress of tumbleweeds.

When hunger pangs roused her the sun was poised like a gold ball over the peak of Mount Adams. She ate her meal and saddled up, riding to the highest ground in the vicinity to study the sunset reddened hills between her and Satus Pass through Duke Perris' field glasses.

Nothing moved on that sage-spiced landscape. If Cleve Logan had been on her tracks, he had lost them in the Pass; that she felt with a definite assurance.

According to the map she had brought from her office, the site of Fort Rimrock was still forty miles away to the east.

She was in no danger of getting lost in these trackless hills; Ringbone's drift fence was a guide on her left and the bleak country was smooth and rolling, promising no canyons or other barriers to night travel.

Giving the roan its head, Opal Waymire pushed on into the heart of the bleak and desolate terrain, fast browning under the summer's heat. Toward dawn a slim sickle of moon put the landscape in harsh relief before her, making it seem doubly formidable and endless.

At midmorning she reached the dry bed of a creek which the map identified as Rattlesnake Creek, which drained this portion of the Horse Heaven watershed into the Columbia.

On the east shoulder of this canyon, where the creek met the gorge, would be the location of Fort Rimrock, which the army had maintained between Fort Walla Walla and Fort Simcoe during the Indian wars.

Hunger and fatigue prompted her to camp in this

defile, but the knowledge that high noon would see her at Perris' rendezvous caused the girl to cross to the far rimrock at the first break which offered itself, and turn directly south.

Being ignorant of this country, she had no way of knowing that the map's paucity of detail had given her no warning of the rough scabrock character of this high mesa, so that the sun was far down before she discerned the squat shape of Fort Rimrock's block-house on the skyline ahead.

The old outpost seemed near enough to touch, its naked rafters etched like black bones against the pearl sky, its loopholes and weather-grayed logs plainly discernible in this crystalline atmosphere.

But, in common with other parts of the west, distances were deceptive and solid objects had a habit of melting into mirage-like forms; and it was a full hour before she sent her tentative halloo toward the ruined blockhouse.

Getting no answer, the girl knew a moment's panic, wondering if Perris and Marengo had somehow failed to find the hideout without a map to guide them.

Then she heard a horse whicker in a stand of cotton-woods around the spring which had been the genesis of this frontier army bastion. As her own mount scented water and broke into a trot, she glimpsed Blackie Marengo's face framed in one of the upper-story loopholes, on lookout duty.

Duke Perris, his jaws covered with a quarter-inch growth of cinnamon stubble, stepped out of the block-house doorway in time to help the dazed and thoroughly wearied girl out of stirrups.

Perris kissed her and carried her into the ruined building, lowering her to a rawhide-latticed bunk which formed the only undamaged furnishings the building offered.

Blackie Marengo swung down a ladder from his lookout post and, bending his lascivious stare on the girl, went out to the waterhole where the girl's roan had plunged its muzzle. He returned a few minutes later with the gunnysacks filled with food and ammunition, to hear Duke Perris explaining their next move.

"We're directly above Winegarten's wood camp and horse ranch," Perris told the girl, who was revivifying herself from the promoter's bottle of whiskey. "We won't wait here any longer than it takes you to rest up and get some food in you. Blackie says he saw a rowboat on the beach by Winegarten's wharf. We'll cross the river tonight and catch ourselves a train on the Oregon side. By tomorrow we'll either be in Portland or Walla Walla."

The three fugitives devoured their meal as full night descended on the Washington hills. Blackie Marengo, always as restless as a panther, saddled their horses for the short ride down to the woodcutter's camp and led them around to the north entrance of the fort.

Myriad stars laid their unearthly beauty over the land and put shadows on the weathered walls of the blockhouse, shedding enough light for Opal Waymire to see the gray trace of the trail which dropped down the steep lava wall into the black unknown of the Columbia.

A thousand feet below the rimrock, a single light

told them the location of the woodcutter's cabin. The shuttering glare of that light and the woodsmoke from Winegarten's chimney touched their nostrils with an earthy, reassuring promise of refuge waiting for them down there.

Opal had brought with her the week's cash receipts of the Palace Casino, amounting to several thousand dollars. Perris transferred that money from her saddle-bags to the carpetbag which had belonged to Jubal Buckring.

"All right," Perris said at length. "We're ready to ride. We're shaking the dust of Washington off our boots a good three days earlier than I'd anticipated."

Saddle gear creaked as Blackie Marengo was the first to mount, moving clumsily because of his broken arm. As Opal settled herself aboard the roan, Duke Perris rounded the rump of his horse and paused to grope for the rawhide thongs which would secure Buckring's carpetbag behind the cantle.

A shooting star made its dissolving spectacular scratch across the zenith. The night breeze whistled its sedative tune through the rafters of the blockhouse overhead. Somewhere down on the river a steamer's whistle reached their ears in distance-thinned ropes of sound.

Perris was in the act of fastening his carpetbag to saddle when a gunshot's flatted roar breached the peacefulness of this night scene, and a bullet thudded into the silvered lintel of the door at his back.

Opal Waymire, alone of the three, located the ambushed rifle beyond the crumbled ruins of an adobe barracks building fifty yards north of the blockhouse.

Her eyes retained the burst of the gun's flash as she sat staring that way, frozen in stirrups by terror.

On the heels of the rifle's slamming echo off the wall of Fort Rimrock came the hoarse but unmistakable voice of Cleve Logan, hidden behind the barrack adobe pile, "Hold it, the three of you. You're surrounded."

As if to prove Logan's words, the heavy bark of a six gun broke from the ebon blot of the trees rimming the waterhole, at a quartering angle from Logan's location. This bullet made its banshee wail over the heads of the trio.

Blackie Marengo was the first to break the paralysis which surprise had put on them.

Wheeling his black mustang sharply, Marengo raked its flanks with steel and rocketed past Opal and Perris, heading for the mesa trail beyond the near corner of the blockhouse.

Hitting the open compound, Marengo drew a responsive crash from Cleve Logan's Winchester. The whack of copper-jacketed lead striking Marengo was a distinct sound to Duke Perris and the girl; they saw the rider rock violently in saddle but recover his balance by clawing the black's mane with his free hand. Wounded, Marengo vanished around the corner of the fort on his stampeding mount, without drawing another shot from the lawman.

Perris' bay reared in panic as the speculator hit the saddle. He kicked Opal's mount to send it stampeding in the direction Blackie had taken, the girl clinging to the pommel to keep from being unhorsed; but, sure target though she was, Logan held his fire.

From his armpit holster Perris jerked a Colt and drove five fast-triggered shots at the barrack ruins to force Logan back. A gun in one hand, Buckring's carpetbag in the other, Perris hooked an elbow around the saddlehorn and leaned Indian-style to the off side of his horse to present a more difficult target.

Before his mount was past the neutral background of the fort wall, in the zone of fire covered by Logan's .45-70, the gun out by the waterhole broke the night's blackness with its orange flame and Perris felt the heavy shock of that following bullet as it drilled his horse in the base of the skull.

The shad-belly bay went down as if a scythe had lopped off its legs in the middle of a stride. Hurled violently from saddle, Perris kicked his Hussar boots free of the oxbow stirrups without conscious volition as he hurtled through space.

He struck the heavy logs of the blockhouse corner with shoulder and skull, and bounced off to lie motionless on the hard-packed gumbo.

Perris' lax fingers still clutched his smoking six gun and the carpetbag of loot which had within it the sum and substance of his long conniving, the lode star he had followed to this ultimate end of his trail.

He was lying like that, without movement and without feeling, when Cleve Logan crossed the starlit compound and squatted over him, hauling Vick Farnick's big handcuffs out of his hip pocket.

"It's all over, Alva!" Logan called to the girl whose

gun had dropped Perris' horse. "We've got to get away from Fort Rimrock before Marengo and Opal come back to side Perris."

21: SKYLINE RIDER

With Perris' limp bulk jack-knifed like a dead man over his shoulder, Logan made his way down into the creek's canyon to where they had left their horses. Alva Ames walked behind them, carrying Perris' money-laden carpetbag; and Logan would never know whether this mild-mannered girl—the daughter and the sister of preachers—had aimed her shot for the rider or the horse back there at the Fort.

From the moment that Alva Ames had caught up with him at the entrance of Satus Pass, Logan had been aware of the futility of trying to persuade the girl against accompanying him on this chase across the Horse Heavens. And Alva had carried her own weight, proving more of an asset than a liability to him.

It was Alva whose sharp gaze had spotted Opal Waymire's distant shape limned against the stars of the Pass summit yesterday, where she had left the stage road without leaving visible clues behind her.

From then on, she had relied on Logan's superior tracking skill and experience to trace the route of Opal Waymire's trek across the hills. What sleep they had had was snatched in saddle; where Opal had camped, they had kept relentlessly on, sparing neither themselves nor their horses.

The grueling toll of this manhunt was on them now,

their bodies crying out for sleep; but Logan knew the danger of being stalked by Blackie Marengo or Opal Waymire, knew the desperate lengths that pair would go to wrest Perris out of his custody.

Perris, his wrist manacles flashing in the starlight, was still unconscious from the effects of the fall he had suffered. Logan boosted him into his own saddle and, forced with the necessity of riding double on their return to Owlhorn, mounted behind the dun's cantle.

It was an hour later, when they gained the west rimrock of the creek's defile, that Logan turned around in saddle to catch a glimpse of a following rider on the skyline between them and Fort Rimrock.

That would be Blackie Marengo, most likely; and the knowledge that they had a desperate gunman on their back trail made Logan more acutely aware than ever of the responsibility he bore to Alva Ames.

Marengo was committed to rescuing Perris before Logan could turn the outlaw over to Marshal Stagman in Owlhorn; not through any great loyalty to Perris, but because of Buckring's money, now in the carpetbag Logan had lashed to his pommel.

In the cold hour of the false dawn, as they were following the Ringbone drift fence toward the west, Logan halted and dismounted to put his ear to the ground. He caught the telegraph of horse's hoofs, and knew that Marengo or Opal, or both, were pressing their pursuit.

"We've got to keep awake," Logan told the girl. "It's possible that Marengo may try cutting around in front of us to pick us off from ambush. I'm sorry, Alva, but that's the way it has to be until Perris is safe in Farnick's jail."

An hour after dawn broke across the Horse Heaven country found them tipping down into a canyon. A trickle of water kept verdure green in this coulee's depths and their horses broke into a stumbling lope as they scented water.

Following Ringbone's fence down into this canyon's cool depths where the sun had not yet penetrated, they smelled woodsmoke and later came in sight of a bearded oldster in a buckskin jacket who was cooking breakfast on a ledge overlooking the stream's pebbled ford.

Duke Perris was conscious now. He spoke no word as he discovered that his legs were roped to stirrups and his wrists manacled with heavy steel bracelets.

At their approach the oldster hobbled out to meet them, waving them away from the clearing in the trees.

"I'm settin' my trap line hyar for coyotes an' timber wolves," he explained, his truculence abating when he spotted the law badge on Logan's shirt. "Can't have the varmints scairt off by man-smell or hoss-smell, so keep out o' this clearin', savvy?"

Logan dragged a hand over his sleep-heavy eyes. "What stream is this?"

The trapper gestured toward the summit. "Source o' Rawhide Crick's up yander a ways."

Logan's eye was on a clearly defined trail which looped off to northward, following the canyon's course.

"Rawhide, you say? That trail leads to Owlhorn?"

The trapper nodded. "If Owlhorn's where you're goin', you'll save twenty-odd mile on that trail, as compared to ridin' west till you hit the Satus road."

Logan turned to Alva. "We'll camp across the creek for a couple hours' sleep," he said. "For you, that is. I have a hunch Marengo may show up here any time now."

The girl nodded indifferently, too far spent to discuss any plans with Logan. For Alva, only the duty of burying her brother could take her back to the Owlhorn she hated. Now that he had Duke Perris in his custody, Logan found himself sharing the girl's aversion to the boom town which had been the scene of the past week's momentous happenings. Along with Perris, Logan would turn over his law star to John Stagman for the last time; already he was eager to get back to his little ranch in the Blue Mountains, and pick up life where he had left it to accept Stagman's assignment of this manhunt.

They crossed the Rawhide and off-saddled, Perris standing by without expression and without speech as Logan spread their saddle-blankets on the pine needles to serve as Alva's bed.

She curled up there and was instantly asleep; and without words of explanation, Logan unlocked Perris' handcuffs, led him over to a loblolly pine snag and, forcing his prisoner to put his arms around the tree's bole, snapped the cuffs over his wrist.

After picketing the horses in a patch of lush bluestem, Logan took his Winchester from scabbard and waded back across the stream to the trapper's camp, his departure watched closely by Perris' bloodshot eyes.

For the better part of the following hour Logan kept his vigil on the far bank, his rifle ready to cover the upper rim should Blackie Marengo appear on the trail there. Off in the clearing, the buckskin-jacketed trapper was busy with his trap-setting, his feet wrapped in gunnysacks to kill the man-spoor.

When Logan returned to their camp on the opposite bank he found Perris asleep, or feigning sleep. Logan untied Buckring's carpetbag from his pommel, opened it to inspect the packets of greenbacks it contained, and then, his face wearing a taut expression, recrossed the Rawhide.

The trapper had packed his belongings on a jenny mule and was preparing to head up-canyon toward the Rawhide's source. He got his parting promise from Logan not to contaminate his trap line, and vanished southerly into the timber.

When he was long gone, Logan went over to the ashes of an old campfire and, digging a hole there, buried Buckring's carpetbag containing Perris' loot, carefully concealing what he had done.

For another hour, Logan fought off sleep while he kept watch on their back trail. He saw no trace of following riders, but he could not be sure that Marengo and Opal had abandoned Perris to concern themselves with their own getaway.

Returning to where Alva and Perris were sleeping, Logan saddled up the horses before rousing the girl and his prisoner.

As they started into the perpetual twilight of the canyon's timber, Alva Ames spoke sharply, "The carpetbag, Cleve. You've lost it somewhere!"

A crooked grin plucked at the corners of Logan's tired mouth as he saw Perris' sharp reaction to the girl's discovery.

"I buried it back down the canyon," Logan said. "We're prime bait for an ambush between here and Owlhorn. If worst comes to worst, at least Marengo won't get the loot. Plenty of time to recover it after Perris is behind bars."

Alva Ames spurred into the lead as the pine-hung trail followed the contours of Rawhide Canyon's twisting course. Whippy undergrowth made riding a tedious business here, making Logan wonder if they had been wise in taking this Owlhorn cut-off.

They had covered another quarter of a mile when Duke Perris, refreshed by his sleep, broke his silence for the first time since his capture.

"You're a dead pigeon and don't know it, Logan. You'll never turn me over to John Stagman tonight."

Before Logan could make answer he saw Alva Ames rein up abruptly, causing Logan's following dun to collide with the paint horse's rump.

Simultaneously a woman's voice lashed sharply out of the dense salal thickets of the trailside, "Put your arms up, Cleve, or Alva's a dead one."

Logan heard Duke Perris' grating laughter echo that voice. At the same instant he caught the subtle fragrance of an alien odor in his nostrils; a woman's expensive perfume.

Then it was that Cleve Logan saw the barrel of the .54 Ballard carbine which was thrust through the oily leaves of the salal, its muzzle aimed inches from Alva Ames' body.

Alva's pinto side-stepped as a Ringbone branded blue roan edged out into the trail, and Cleve Logan saw the dappled sunlight and shadow playing on the gaunt, twisted face of Opal Waymire.

Opal, then, and not Blackie Marengo, had been the unseen stalker who had pursued them from Fort Rimrock. To buck Opal's cold drop now meant sure death for Alva Ames. That knowledge brought Cleve Logan's hands away from his reins, holding them high.

"Hold your trigger, Opal," Logan said heavily. "You've dealt yourself all the aces here."

Opal's lips moved tautly, "Step down, Cleve. I want you to unlock Duke's handcuffs."

Twisting around in her saddle to meet Logan's eye, Alva Ames knew that the man had no choice in this catastrophic situation. She read the full measure of Logan's despair as he slid backwards off the dun's rump, Opal's rifle following him.

"Unbuckle your gunbelt," the honkytonk girl continued in her listless monotone.

The Ballard had swung back to cover Alva now; and Logan, knowing the nervous pressure Opal was under, made no delay in removing his Colt harness and tossing it into the brush.

Duke Perris, in the act of dismounting, said sharply

to Opal, "Don't shoot Logan yet. He got rid of Buck-ring's carpetbag further down the canyon."

Perris held out his shackled arms as Logan got the sheriff's key from his pocket and unlocked his prisoner's handcuffs.

As soon as he was free Perris snatched the heavy irons from Logan's grasp and notched them on the lawman's wrists. Removing the key from one of the cuffs, Perris hurled it far out through the trees.

"You'll not be needing that key," Perris laughed, stepping over to Alva's horse and reaching up to remove the girl's gun from its holster on her saddle fender. "Climb down, Alva."

The girl dismounted stiffly, moving like a sleeper in the coils of a nightmare. She was well aware, even as was Logan, that Opal Waymire's circling around in front of them to trap them here could have but one outcome—doom for both of them.

"See why I stashed your loot like I did, Perris?" Logan said bitterly, as the speculator thrust the muzzle of Alva's gun into his belly. "Pull that trigger and you lose everything you had at stake in Owlhorn. So you won't shoot, will you, Duke?"

Perris stepped back, leaving Opal to keep Logan under the pointblank menace of her carbine.

Turning, Perris hefted the .44 in his hand and swung it inches from Alva's midriff.

"Tell me where you cached that bag, Logan," Perris ordered in a venomous whisper, "or I'll drop this girl in her tracks. It's up to you."

It was Opal Waymire who broke the following silence.

"No, Duke. You couldn't kill a woman."

Perris' heated face turned a shade darker, to match the crusted blood stains on his gashed scalp.

"This is no time for sentimentality, Opal. It was Alva who brought about my capture at the Fort last night. Do you think I'd leave Alva Ames behind with her knowing I killed Logan? With her knowing I shot her brother?"

Logan saw the shock and frustration cross Alva's face at this cold-blooded confession of Jebediah's bushwhacking.

"All right, Duke," Logan cut in hoarsely, seeing Perris' trigger finger whitening at the knuckle joint. "I'm ready to bargain with you. I'll take you to where I buried Jubal Buckring's carpetbag on condition that you leave Alva free to ride out of here. Wherever you and Opal will go, you'll never leave a trail Alva could follow."

Crafty changes occurred in Perris' eyes as he pondered this proposition. Finally he turned to Opal.

"I'll take up Logan on that offer," he said. "Get his rope off the saddle yonder and tie Alva to that spruce snag yonder. When the carpetbag is in our hands, we can ride back here and set her afoot. We'll be in Oregon before she can reach the sheriff in Owlhorn with her story."

Opal Waymire swung out of stirrups, cradled her rifle under one arm and walked over to Logan's horse, taking down the coil of lass' rope from the pommel. Logan saw by the stricken gravity in the girl's face that she sensed the underlying treachery back of

Perris' quick acceptance of Logan's terms.

Once Buckring's money was in their hands, Perris would return to this lonely spot and put a bullet through Alva's trussed-up body. Even Opal Waymire did not have enough influence over this desperate and ruthless man to prevent him from destroying this sole remaining witness to his perfidy.

If Alva suspected her danger, she gave no sign of it as she walked over to a lightning-charred spruce snag and let Opal truss her to the tree, her arms surrounding the silver trunk.

When Opal had finished Duke Perris walked over to check Alva's bonds. Then he mounted the girl's pinto, gesturing with his gun for Cleve Logan to mount.

When Logan was in saddle Perris spurred forward and stooped to grab the dun's reins.

Sitting there, boxed in by his two captors, Cleve Logan flexed his manacled hands and spoke softly to Alva:

"I'm a bit late in telling you this, Alva, but my love is yours and has been ever since you helped me board the *Sacajawea* that time. In case I don't get back to put it a little better."

Alva's choked reply was lost under the abrasive scrape of hoofs as Duke Perris, leading Logan's dun, headed off down the winding canyon trail, Opal Waymire bringing up the rear.

Watching that cavalcade vanish around the coulee's bend, Alva Ames knew then that she would never see Cleve Logan alive this side of eternity; his declaration of love for her had been his farewell, his requiem for what would never be.

As they reached the ford where they had made their brief camp, Duke Perris reined around in saddle to break the silence of their ride. "You didn't go far from here to hide that carpetbag, Logan. If you think you can double-cross me this late in the game—"

Logan shook his head.

"I cached it over on the other bank," he said heavily. "Do you think I'd buck this thing out with Alva's life at forfeit?"

Relief showed on the hard lines of Duke Perris' jaw as they headed across the ripples of the Rawhide and reined up at the edge of the little clearing where the drowned remains of the trapper's campfire made a gray smudge on the dirt.

Logan dismounted here, the sunlight flashing on the nickeled bracelets at his wrists. Opal Waymire remained in saddle, the Ballard .54 balanced across her pommel, as Duke Perris stepped down from Alva's pinto and lifted his six gun.

"Lead off," he ordered. "You understand, Logan, even after Buckring's money is in my hands there's no way out for you?"

Logan's shoulders lifted and fell, indicative of his own abandoned hopes.

Turning to Opal, the deputy marshal said bleakly, "I'm depending on you to make sure Alva isn't left up there to starve."

He saw Opal nod, but he knew from the tragic line

of her mouth that she was under no illusions as to how events would run after Logan had been added to the list of Perris' victims. To Duke Perris, Opal was just another woman to love and abandon; if Perris had made up his mind to murder Alva Ames, nothing she could do would prevent that treachery.

Logan plodded out into the center of the campground area and stood staring around at the mottled smudges of old campfires. He walked over to one, studying it carefully, and then touched it with a boot toe.

"The carpetbag is down there, buried a foot under those ashes, Perris."

Perris came forward warily, staring at the ashes, noting where they had been fanned out smooth by a waved hatbrim, obliterating the stippled formation which a recent rain had put on the surrounding earth.

"You aim to kill me," Logan went on, "so go ahead with it. What are you waiting for?"

Perris looked up, his eyes aglitter.

"You think I'd shoot first and do my treasure hunting afterward? I'm not that dense a fool, Logan. No. I'll make sure you've given me the right information."

Logan stood there, his jaw slumped on his chest.

Behind him he heard Opal spurring her horse closer.

Duke Perris got down on his knees, laying the cocked six gun carefully to one side. His nugget watch chain dangled down from his chest, the gold bullet ornament swaying like a pendulum, its dazzling spears of light twinkling on the gray ashes.

"If the bag isn't buried here," Perris said, "I won't waste time arguing with you, Logan. There's a few Indian tricks to make a man loosen his tongue."

Logan grunted. "I know that, knowing you. Go ahead and dig. I have nothing to gain by stalling you with a wrong steer."

Perris brushed aside the charcoal and stubs of firewood and cowchips to thrust his hooked fingers into the powdery ashes, digging like a spaniel after a marrow bone.

A grin broke the strained absorption of Perris' face as he came to the ground level and knew by the broken clods that Logan had not lied, that a hole had been dug through the hardpan recently.

Dust and ashes fumed up to cloud Perris' sweating cheeks as he pawed deeper into that loose earth, fingernails scratching aside ashes and dirt, his senses tingling from the anticipation of uncovering the treasure-laden carpetbag.

Opal Waymire watched from saddle, sharing the outlaw's mounting excitement.

It came without warning—a geysering burst of loose earth and white ashes, timed with a metallic clang as if some buried spring had exploded under the campfire's remains.

A bellow of blended pain and fear came from Duke Perris as he lurched up on his knees, to reveal the notched iron jaws of a Number Four wolf trap clamped deep in the flesh of his left hand, midway between wrist and knuckles, the heavy metal teeth sunk cruelly into bone and tendon. Connected to that heavy trap was a short length of chain fastened to an iron peg driven deep in the ground.

Overcome as he was by surprise and the agony of his mangled hand, Duke Perris was aware of Logan's trick and his right hand moved by pure reflex toward the gun he had laid to one side in handy reach for emergency.

Logan's shadow was a fast moving blur as, timed with the trap's violent jump out of the loose earth which had buried it, he launched himself in a dive at Duke Perris, ignoring the threat of Opal Waymire's waiting gun at his back.

Handicapped by the steel fetters on his wrist, Logan knew he had no chance to beat Perris' reach for the gun. His spike-heeled cowboot stamped the outlaw's fingers in the act of coiling around the rubber-stocked butt of that weapon, a following kick sending the six-shooter skidding off to one side.

With a bull-like roar springing from deep in his lungs, Perris came half to his feet, only to be jerked to his knees by the snapped tautness of the trap's chain.

He saw Opal lifting her rifle to cover Logan, and Perris' shout came with a frenzied appeal, "Shoot, Opal, damn you!"

For a long instant Opal Waymire held Logan's back in her sights as the deputy threw himself clear of Perris and made his pounce for the six gun. But her finger was frozen on the trigger as she saw Logan's manacled hands scoop up the Colt and whirl like an animal at bay.

Perris' free hand made its stabbing motion to the

flared top of one of his Hussar bootlegs and came out with a short-barreled .41 derringer, a hideout weapon which Logan, in his haste to leave Fort Rimrock in the darkness of last night, had failed to discover.

Logan saw eternity yawning in the big bore of that derringer as he brought up his clumsily-grasped Colt and snapped the gunhammer.

Simultaneously with the roar of the .44 in Logan's hands a spurt of flame flicked from Perris' tiny weapon, but the lethal slug hit the dirt between Logan's widespread legs.

A fount of blood spurted from the bullet hole which was punched through Duke Perris' throat. That blood showered down over his dusty fustian coat and ran down the node of his watch chain to drip off the gold bullet luck piece during the full twenty seconds Perris remained in his half-erect posture.

Death's close approach was glazing Perris' eyes as he pulled Opal Waymire's face into focus.

"You had your chance and let Logan live," Perris said with a ghastly exhalation. "I didn't know that's how the cards lay."

Opal Waymire let the big Ballard carbine drop to the ground as she saw Duke Perris topple sidewise and lie still. She leaped from saddle and ran to Perris' side, cradling the man's blood-stained head against the soft swell of her breast.

She was crooning softly, rocking the man's head slowly in her arms as a mother might comfort a child, when Perris' body jerked in its final paroxysm and lay lax against her.

Not until he had his proof that life was extinct in the man who had been the object of his manhunt west did Cleve Logan tip his six gun toward the sky and ease down the knurled hammer.

He knew Opal Waymire's acute need to be left alone in this moment of communion with the man whose life she could easily have saved, but had not. But there was something he had to know and he put his question in the quietest voice.

"Is Marengo with you, Opal?"

She looked up, something infinitely lovely showing through the sagging tissues of her cheeks. "No, Cleve. I found Blackie dead, below the mesa at Fort Rimrock. Your bullet had gone clean through him."

He whispered "So," and felt no regrets.

Sensing the depths of the woman's grief and dawning self-condemnation, realizing something of the poignant reason which lay behind the break she had given him, Logan walked over to pick up the girl's rifle and continued on across this campground to halt beside the still-wet ashes of the campfire which the old trapper had drowned this morning.

He stooped to dig in the ashes there, and brought to light Jubal Buckring's carpetbag.

He hung the bag on the dun's saddlehorn and turned to where Opal Waymire knelt, sobbing openly as she pressed a cheek against the dead man's temple, a beringed hand gently stroking Perris' stubbled chin.

Logan said nothing until he had put a boot heel on the wolf trap and freed Perris' dead hand from its clamping jaws.

"What Perris didn't know," he said gently, "was that I watched that trapper set his traps under several of these campfires around here. It's an old trick trappers use, knowing wild animals will invariably dig around a campfire in search of garbage."

Through flooding eyes, Opal Waymire watched Logan empty her rifle and return it to its scabbard under her saddle skirt. Glancing down at his braceleted hands, he said bleakly, "If the sheriff hasn't got a duplicate key to these irons I'll have to visit a blacksmith when I get back to town."

Opal Waymire reverently lowered Perris' head to the ground, turning to look at Logan with eyes wholly devoid of emotion.

"At least," she said, "you'll have one prisoner to turn over to John Stagman tonight."

Logan shook his head, drawing a flicker of incredulity from the dead, lost depths of Opal Waymire's eyes.

"I reckon not, Opal," he said gently. "Losing the man you loved is punishment you'll carry always. Let's say I'm squaring my debt to you. I realize what it meant for you to hold your fire just now."

The girl turned back, running her fingers through Perris' short-cropped hair. Without looking up she said, "Tell Alva not to think too harshly of me, Cleve. My last wish is for your happiness together. You see, I love you, Cleve."

In the act of mounting, Logan was caught and held by the intonation in Opal Waymire's words. The morbid finality of her tone caused Logan to walk over

234

to her horse, checking the contents of the gunnysacks lashed behind her cantle.

He found a loaded Remington .45 and jacked it open, spilled five cartridges into his hand, and made certain no other ammunition of that caliber was in the sacks.

Then, as an afterthought, he removed the cylinder and threw it far out into Rawhide Creek. Opal Waymire's eyes followed the arc of the gun's cylinder, marking with a bright calculation the silvery geyser it made where it hit the ford.

"I'll tell Alva," he said, lifting his Stetson to the girl who waited beside Duke Perris. "So long, Opal. I'm sorry the way things worked out for you."

He caught the trailing reins of Alva's paint horse and rode away, crossing the Rawhide ford and disappearing into the further trees, leaving Opal alone with her grief.

Long after the sound of Cleve Logan's departure had faded down-canyon, Opal Waymire sat beside the dead man, her eyes fixed with a macabre fascination on the gold cartridge which Duke Perris had worn as a luck charm as long as she had known him.

Getting to her feet, Opal Waymire moved like a person in a drugged trance, over to her horse. She found the dismantled Remington revolver where Logan had left it in a gunnysack, and, hugging the gun to her, ran across the campground to wade into the Rawhide's platinum ripples.

Sunlight picked out the furbished blued-steel surfaces of the Remington's cylinder lying under a foot of water on the pebbly bed. She retrieved it, wiped it dry on the hem of her riding habit and fitted it back into the gun's frame.

Returning to where Duke Perris lay, she knelt and with fingers which held no slightest suggestion of tremor, removed the clip which attached Duke Perris' luck charm to the blood-sticky watch chain.

She slipped the golden bullet into a chamber of the Remington's cylinder, saw the cartridge case seat its flange snugly under the firing pin.

All the pathos and tenderness which this woman had ever known for this man who had used her so selfishly through the years of their lives together stormed to the surface of Opal's heart as she pressed the gun's muzzle under her left breast.

She looked into Perris' dead face and moved her lips in a soundless whisper.

"We belong together, Duke. We'll always be together—"

Cleve Logan was putting his horse around the last bend of the rocky trail through the conifers when the single muffled crash of a gunshot followed him down the cliff-walled gulch.

The slamming echoes of that shot caused him to rein up the horses sharply, pulling around in the direction of the camp. His brows were pulled together with a stunned wonderment as to where and how he could have slipped up in his precautions, knowing as he did the resolve of self-destruction which had ruled Opal Waymire at the moment of their parting.

"Perris' gold bullet," he said finally, as understanding came to him. "I overlooked that. Never was sure whether that trinket was a dummy or not."

He put the dun into a gallop, thrusting Opal Waymire and Duke Perris out of his mind. Rounding the bend in the narrow trail, he saw Alva's face turned toward him from her position with her back to the lightning-struck spruce, a pencil of golden sunlight slanting off the rimrock to put blue glints in her raven hair.

He pulled the horses in fast at the base of the snag and dismounted, tarrying only to rummage his saddlebag for the stockman's knife he kept there. As the lariat parted under the thrusts of that razor-honed blade, Alva Ames fell forward against him.

Logan lifted his manacled wrists over her head and down behind her shoulders, pulling her hard against him. She spoke then, all her heart's desire in her voice for him to claim.

"I love you dearly, Cleve. As long as I shall live you are mine to cherish and I am yours for whatever lies ahead."

Their lips melted in the kiss that sealed the common destiny they would share throughout the future. They clung to this moment, savoring it hungrily, knowing that for them life would never hold another moment as magic as this one which found them standing together at the open door of their most secret dreams.

For these two, Logan's ranch in the Blue Mountains would be the place which the children Alva would bear him would learn to know as the hills of home.

Center Point Publishing
600 Brooks Road ● PO Box 1
Thorndike ME 04986-0001 USA

(207) 568-3717

US & Canada:
1 800 929-9108